Harry refilled my glass. "I bet you're good at human-interest stories," he said.

"I hope so," I answered. "At any rate, I'm going to give it a try. Since there don't seem to be that many kids our age traveling around Spain this time of year, I feel a little more optimistic. Have you ever heard of Barbara Channing?"

Harry bent to pick up the napkin that had slid from his lap. "Sure." His voice sounded muffled.

"Well, Uncle Frank's very keen to get the inside story on her divorce. I have to track down her son and induce him to tell all. He's supposed to be traveling in Spain right now, probably under an assumed name."

"If he's not using his real name, how will you know when you've found him?"

"Intuition. Logic. Deduction. I haven't worked out all the details yet...."

Dear Readers:

Thank you for your unflagging interest in First Love From Silhouette. Your many helpful letters have shown us that you have appreciated growing and stretching with us, and that you demand more from your reading than happy endings and conventional love stories. In the months to come we will make sure that our stories go on providing the variety you have come to expect from us. We think you will enjoy our unusual plot twists and unpredictable characters who will surprise and delight you without straying too far from the concerns that are very much part of all our daily lives.

We hope you will continue to share with us your ideas about how to keep our books your very First Loves. We depend on you to keep us on our toes!

Nancy Jackson
Senior Editor
FIRST LOVE FROM SILHOUETTE

CASTLES IN SPAIN
Janice Harrell

First Love from Silhouette

Published by Silhouette Books New York

America's Publisher of Contemporary Romance

SILHOUETTE BOOKS
300 E. 42nd St., New York, N.Y. 10017

ISBN: 0-373-06224-9

First Silhouette Books printing February 1987

America's Publisher of Contemporary Romance

Printed in the U.S.A.

RL 6.1, IL age 11 and up

First Love from Silhouette by Janice Harrell

Puppy Love #67
Heavens to Bitsy #95
Secrets in the Garden #128
Killebrew's Daughter #134
Sugar n' Spice #159
Blue Skies and Lollipops #165
Birds of a Feather #187
With Love from Rome #205
Castles in Spain #224

JANICE HARRELL is the eldest of five children and spent her high school years in the small, central Florida town of Ocala. She earned her B.A. at Eckerd College and her M.A. and Ph.D. from the University of Florida. For a number of years she taught English at the college level. She now lives with her husband and their young daughter.

Chapter One

Saturday afternoon, I was perched on a low stool in an aisle of the library, planning a trip to Europe. I knew that the only trip I was ever likely to get was the one my family took every year to Myrtle Beach, but that didn't stop me. I was writing out my itinerary on a notepad. "Paris," I began. Then I chewed on my pencil. Should I take the express train from Paris to Rome? Or should I wander down through Spain and take a tramp steamer from there to Naples? I studied the European railroad timetable that I had balanced on one knee and decided on the tramp steamer. I'd meet more interesting people that way. Bullfighters, maybe. Or spies. I didn't have a steamer timetable, but I could work out the details when I got there. *If* I got there.

I pushed that unwelcome thought from my mind and tried to concentrate on my itinerary. After Rome, maybe I'd go to Venice and ride on a gondola. Thinking of myself in a gondola drifting past the crumbling old palaces of Venice, I gave a contented sigh. I loved planning trips to Europe. I even loved the shelves at the back of the library where they put the travel books. No one seemed to come back there much but me. I could sit there in peace surrounded by dust and my favorite books, like *Travel on a Shoestring* and *I Was a Teenage Vagabond*. Another good one was *So You Want To Be in the Foreign Service*. That was the one that had given me the idea of signing up for Spanish. Languages would be important in the Foreign Service.

Not that I was absolutely set on the Foreign Service. What I was set on was getting out of Hockley, North Carolina. In Hockley there was a definite shortage of bullfighters and spies. In fact, there was a definite shortage of anything whatever that was interesting. An alert and adventurous young mind like mine could wither away from lack of stimulation. It was a possibility I brooded about a lot.

I leaned back against the book stack and imagined myself moving through Europe on a speeding train. As we sped along, suddenly a famous artist in a black beret pushed his way through the beaded curtains that separated the coach from the club car, caught sight of me and cried hoarsely, "That face! I must paint it!" I was vaguely aware that beaded curtains might not be standard issue on today's trains and that there was probably nothing about my heart-shaped face and fluffy short brown hair that would make any artist want to paint me, but since it was my fantasy, I figured I could arrange it any way I liked.

Just then my daydream was disturbed by the sound of heavy footsteps. I looked up and was not surprised to see my friend Rosemary. It was always nice to hear

Rosemary coming because she was not very graceful. In fact, she was the classic case of somebody who walked like two men carrying a ladder. She did, however, have nice auburn hair pulled straight back from her face and falling down her back.

"Is this the travel section?" she whispered.

"Sure," I said. I didn't point out that if I was sitting there it *had* to be the travel section. I preferred to keep secret my love for this particular row of books. Even I could see it was a little flaky to spend my spare time at the library planning trips I couldn't possibly take. "Looking for anything special?" I asked.

"A book about Spain," she said.

I reached out my left hand and unerringly put it on James Michener's *Iberia*. I knew right where it was, natch. I knew where everything in the travel section was. I hoisted it off the shelf with some effort and handed it to her.

She looked at it doubtfully. "It's awfully big."

"Spain's a big country," I said. As she leafed through it, I hesitated. Should I ask her why she wanted a book about Spain? Maybe she was writing a report. I hoped that was it because if Rosemary was getting to go to Spain, I was just going to die of jealousy, that's all. I cleared my throat. "Need it for anything in particular?" I asked.

She beamed at me. Obviously, she had been panting for me to ask. "I'm going to get to go to Spain!" she said. "Mom and Dad already said I could. Guess what, Cassie? Mr. Hinson is taking a bunch of kids to Spain for two weeks over Thanksgiving break."

"Mr. Hinson our Spanish teacher?"

"Right! Back when he was teaching in Pennsylvania, he used to take a busload of kids to Spain every year, but this is the first time he's done it since he came to Hockley." She looked smug. "It's going to be very educational. That's what Mom and Dad liked about the idea."

"How much?" I asked in hollow tones.

"Only $1,500. A real bargain."

Fifteen hundred dollars might be a real bargain to Rosemary, but to me it was a real impossibility. I was finally able to manage a weak smile. "You'll send me a postcard, won't you?"

"Oh, come on, Cassie! Why don't you go, too? If you did we could room together."

It had its comical side. Rosemary was actually trying to *persuade* me to go to Europe. But fifteen hundred dollars! Where could I ever come up with money like that?

"I'm sure you could get the money somewhere," she said, reading my mind. "What about that summer job you've got lined up? You could borrow against that."

She seemed to have an exaggerated idea of what I was going to be able to earn dishing up burgers part-time. I figured I would only make about seven hundred dollars and my parents had already hinted that the money ought to be saved for college.

Still, a little flame of excitement flickered inside me in spite of myself. This was my chance, my first chance to actually get out of Hockley and into the big, exciting world outside. Also it was a chaperoned, educational-type trip, something I was sure my parents would let me do if I could only come up with the cash.

"Oh, come on, Cassie," pleaded Rosemary. "I'm afraid I'm going to end up rooming with a couple of strangers. Mr. Hinson told Dad only about half of the kids come from his Spanish classes. The others will be kids from other schools, kids we don't even know. I could get stuck with somebody awful."

I was unwilling to admit my case was hopeless. "Maybe I can think up some way to manage it," I said slowly.

"We could have the most fantastic time! Just think of it! Spain!"

I was afraid if I started thinking about it I would get so excited I would lose consciousness. I had better concentrate on the money problem instead. That would keep me down to earth.

When I got home I took out a sheet of paper and wrote "$1500" at the top of it. I thought I could persuade my parents to advance me seven hundred against my summer job earnings. They might prefer for me to save the money for college, but a trip to Spain would be, after all, an educational experience and sort of like college, so I substracted seven hundred from the total. Then I looked at the still awesome amount remaining with a feeling of growing gloom.

I went to get my savings passbook out of my jewelry box and considered my total cash assets—seventy-five dollars. That wouldn't make much of a dent in the eight hundred I still needed. I picked up the diamond ring Grandma had left me in her will and fingered it, wondering what I would get if I hocked it. Then I put it back in the jewelry box and closed the thing up quickly. I had the uneasy feeling that Grandma was watching me from somewhere and was disapproving. I couldn't help wishing that when her things had been parceled out she had left the diamond ring to Matt and given me the cash instead of vice versa. If I had that cash, I would have known just what to do with it.

When I once more stared at my sheet of figures, every travel book I had ever read seemed to pass before my eyes—books about crossing the Alps on a bicycle, books about canoe trips down the Irawaddy, books on safaris and on caravan travel—I had read them all. Then I found myself imagining a book with me actually in it. I could see it clearly—*Castles in Spain* by Catherine (aka Cassie) Wilkerson, Footloose Press, 1986.

Suddenly my idea came to me. I *could* be in a travel book. Why not? I would write it myself. I knew how it was done. I had certainly read enough of them. The important thing was that I had some ready-made readers. I could sell it to the kids taking the trip with me! I envisioned a simple printing job, offset printing, maybe, done right from my typescript and my picture layout. Because, of course, it would have heaps of pictures to make it more appealing to the reader. I would bind it with a couple of plain ring binders and light cardboard. It would be cheap to print and I figured I could sell the copies for ten dollars each. For once, I was glad that my father ran a struggling print shop instead of being a bank president. Surely he would give his own daughter a break on the price of the printing, wouldn't he?

Clutching my page of figures, I dashed into the family room to find Dad. He was immersed in a magazine, a cloud of smoke from his pipe almost enveloping his head.

"Where's Matt?" I asked.

"He's gone over to Mickey's, I think. You need him for something?"

"No!" I said quickly. "I just need to talk to you and Mom." I could see that presenting my ideas to Mom and Dad might be delicate. I didn't need to have my brother piping in with sarcastic remarks just when I was making my best points.

Mom heard me and came into the family room. "What's up, Cassie?"

"Guess what, Mom! My Spanish teacher, Mr. Hinson, is taking a tour group of kids to Spain over Thanksgiving!"

They managed to contain their excitement.

"It's going to be properly chaperoned and extremely educational and it's only going to cost fifteen hundred dollars for two weeks." Dad took his pipe out of his mouth, and I was afraid he was going to object so I rushed on. "I think I've just about worked out how to pay for it, too. I'm going to earn about seven hundred dollars on my job at Quick Burger. If you could just advance me that money I could pay you back this summer. It would really be worth it because it would be so educational and an extremely valuable experience for a person who is considering a career in the Foreign Service."

"It sounds very nice, sweetheart," said Mom, "and I wish we could do it for you, but you know we don't have the money to spend on something like that."

"You'd only have to *lend* me the seven hundred, not give it to me," I pointed out. "And I have another idea, too." I outlined my terrific plans for writing a book about the trip to be sold to the participants. To my relief, they seemed to be listening to me seriously.

Dad took the pipe from his mouth. "How much do you think you could clear on the book?" he asked.

"I think about four hundred, less the printing costs, of course."

"I'd give you the printing," he said. "But the problem is, you need the money for the books up front. You can't just make up these books and hope somebody buys them. You've got to be sure they're bought before you sign up for the trip. What if only a few kids want the book? You'd be in the soup. And have you thought about postage costs? If half the kids are going to come from other schools, the way you say, you're going to need to mail them the book after it's printed."

Mom pulled my page of figures over toward her and looked at them. "But even if we advance you your summer money, sweetheart, and even if your book goes over with a bang, you're still short four hundred dollars."

"I've got seventy-five dollars in the bank," I said quickly.

"But you're going to need some spending money. And I'd be surprised if every single item is included in the fifteen hundred dollars. Do you know for a fact that it covers the meals, for example?"

"I don't mind skipping meals," I said. "I don't eat much, anyway."

"I know you really want to go," she said, "and we sympathize, don't we, Bob? But you're going to have to come up with some more money. It would be all we could do to advance you that money against your summer job."

"I just know I can come up with it somehow," I said, gritting my teeth.

"When do you have to tell them whether you're going?" said Mom.

"I'm not sure. Mr. Hinson is going to talk to the class about it Monday, and I suppose I'll find out then."

"It's a lot of money," said Mom, shaking her head.

A few minutes later, Mom dragged Dad off to help her put up a new spice rack in the kitchen, and I flopped down on the couch thinking desperate thoughts.

Four hundred dollars! Mom was right. It was a lot of money. I wondered what I would get if I sold all my bedroom furniture and just slept on the floor from now on. Probably not enough.

I idly picked up *Vision*, the magazine Dad had been reading. My uncle Frank was the managing editor, which was one reason we subscribed to it. Of course, most other American households subscribed to it, too. Consequently, its budget was enormous. Uncle Frank's reporters thought nothing of renting helicopters and cruisers and tons of electronic flash equipment in their pursuit of a hot news story. Four hundred dollars was peanuts to a magazine like *Vision*. I wondered if they would like to make a donation to the education of a struggling young girl. Reluctantly, I decided it was not likely. Uncle Frank was one of the most hard-bitten guys in the world. I doubted that he even bought Girl Scout cookies.

On the other hand, what did I have to lose? I asked myself. Four hundred dollars wasn't going to materialize if I just sat there on the sofa feeling sorry for myself.

I quietly sneaked back into Mom and Dad's bedroom and dialed New York. Uncle Frank answered the phone with his usual unintelligible bark.

"Uncle Frank?" I said. "This is Cassie. No, everything's fine. Yes, Mom and Dad are fine." Uncle Frank's steady coverage of earthquakes, famine and flood had left him with a permanently downbeat outlook on life. "No everything's all right, really. I only called because there's a chance I might get to go to

Spain for two weeks in November and I wondered if you'd like to buy a story about a teenager's first trip to Europe. I'd sell it to you cheap and I'd do all the pictures myself.''

His laugh was so loud that I had to hold the phone away from my ear. I didn't see why he had to roar like that. A simple no, thank you would have done. Finally he pulled himself together. ''The photographic standards of a magazine like *Vision* are extraordinarily high, Cassie,'' he said. ''We don't publish snapshots. And as for the text blocks, writing them is a good deal harder than it looks. Now tell me, how's the family? Is Bob's back still acting up?''

''No, everything's fine,'' I said. I considered trying to persuade him that my photography was up to a professional standard and that my text blocks would be super. But I could see he was prejudiced against my idea and that it was hopeless. I was also conscious that my long-distance bill was mounting up, which might cause questions when Mom was going over the phone bill next month. ''I'd better go now,'' I said.

''Nice talking to you, Cassie,'' he said in a phony jovial voice. ''Believe me, I'm honored that you thought of *Vision*, but it's not a story we can use.''

''It was just an idea,'' I said. ''So long.''

I hung up the phone, gritting my teeth. Boy, would I like to show him. Would I like to have the story of the century and sell it to a rival magazine! Would I like to win the Pulitzer Prize and wave it in his face!

Get a grip on yourself, Cassie, I told myself. So your idea of selling a story to *Vision* bombed. There must be some other way you can dig up four hundred dollars.

Just then, I heard Matt come in the front door. Matt had four hundred dollars, that legacy from Grandma.

I found him in the family room switching on the television. "Hey, Matt," I said, "how would you like for me to go away for two whole weeks?"

He looked at me suspiciously. "What's the catch?"

"I just need to borrow four hundred dollars. I've got a chance to go to Spain with my Spanish class and I've got all the money lined up except for four hundred dollars. What do you say?"

"I'd charge interest."

"That's okay."

"Twenty percent."

"Twenty percent!" I screeched.

"It's a high-risk loan. Heck, you could get hit by a car over there. You never look both ways."

"I do so."

"You do not. Anyway, that's my price. Take it or leave it."

"I take it," I said.

"And don't tell Mom and Dad about the interest, either."

"Okay."

"And if you don't pay me back I'm going to fry your liver in oil. I get my money at the end of the summer, right?"

"Not exactly. I need this summer's money for paying Mom and Dad back for the money they're lending me. But I could pay you back the summer after that."

Matt's eyes glittered as he figured the return on a twenty percent loan over two years. I was selling myself into peonage, I knew, but I *had* to get to Spain.

"Okay," he said. "But you've got to give me Grandma's ring as security and I want you to sign a real promissory note."

"No problem," I said. I had already quit worrying about the twenty percent and was imagining myself climbing the winding stairs of a castle in Spain. I was going to Europe! I was actually going! It was unbelievable. I waltzed out of the room.

Now all I had to do was to persuade Mr. Hinson to back my book. I was a little worried about how to go about it since my whole plan hinged on it. But as it turned out, it was easy to persuade him. The next day, after church, I saw him at the social hour and put the idea to him. To my surprise, he was very enthusiastic. He was sure the book would be great and said he only wished he had thought of doing something like that for the past bunch of trips he had organized because it would have made it that much easier to get this one off the ground. He loved the idea of sending copies to Spanish teachers as a promotional idea. I should have known that a man who was willing to be responsible for thirty kids in a foreign country was not the type to make petty objections. Mr. Hinson was a natural optimist.

Rosemary called me that afternoon. "Well, how's it going?" she asked. "Do you think you can go?"

"I think so," I said, my heart knocking against my chest at the very thought of it.

"Whee!" said Rosemary.

Chapter Two

Monday, when Mr. Hinson told our Spanish class about the trip, I was alarmed to see that nobody seemed to be jotting down the information about the meeting he was having on it. After class I grabbed Rosemary in a panic-stricken grip. "What if he cancels the trip for lack of interest?"

She detached my fingers from her shirt sleeves. "Keep calm, Cassie. There are lots of other Spanish classes besides ours. There are the second- and third-year kids, too. Besides, I know for a fact that Lolita's parents have said she can go. That's three of us already. And there'll be those kids from other schools."

"You're right," I said. "I'm getting too wrought up about this. I've got to keep calm." But it wasn't easy. I was so close to getting to go that I knew I couldn't stand it if there was a snag now.

Mom went with me to the meeting about the trip. I was relieved to see that the room was full of people, after all. Mr. Hinson showed slides of Spain and talked about the special lectures we would get on things like the history and art of Spain. Then he got down to the really gritty things like when the first deposit money had to be in, how our school work could be made up and how much luggage we could carry. "Sixty-pound limit," he said. "And keep in mind that you will have to carry it everywhere yourself, so you would be wise to make it much, much less."

After the meeting I was shivering with excitement. I was really going to go! Me—Cassie—I was going to Europe. Rosemary, on the other hand, was still worrying about the roommate problem.

"You heard him say we'll be three to a room," she said. "We've got to get ourselves another roommate. What about Lolita?"

"It's okay with me," I said. I thrust my hands in my jacket pockets and did a cheerful little pirouette.

"I think we'd better pack some crackers and candy and some instant coffee," said Rosemary. "You know, all the food is going to be foreign over there."

"It's *supposed* to be foreign, idiot," I said.

Behind me I could hear our mothers talking. "Of course, I trust Rosemary implicitly," said Rosemary's mother. "She's very responsible."

Instead of chiming in that she trusted me equally well, Mom said, "It's nice to know that the Hinsons will keep an eye on them."

"What a fantastic educational experience it will be," burbled Mrs. Townsend. "I wish I had had an opportunity like this when I was young. They'll learn so much about history, art, culture. And soon they'll be chattering away in Spanish. There's nothing like going to a country to help you with the language, I always say."

"Elise Hinson told me that she and Bernie have taken eight busloads of kids to Spain and they've never had a bit of trouble," Mom put in anxiously.

I was beginning to wonder if Mom *suspected* I had a yen for adventure.

"Oh, look!" said Rosemary. "There's Lolita. Let's hurry. Catch her before she gets out the door."

We ran over together to intercept Lolita. She looked like a midget walking next to her dad. But then Lolita was short by anybody's standards, a small black girl with her hair in a French twist and a dazzling white smile that was a first-class advertisement for her dad the dentist.

"Lolita, how'd you like to room with Cassie and me?" Rosemary said breathlessly.

"Sounds good," said Lolita.

"We're going. We're really going!" I said, jumping up and down. "Isn't it exciting?"

"Don't pay any attention to her," said Rosemary. "She's been like that for days."

"I can't wait," said Lolita. "I'm going to buy me one of those mantilla things and put a rose between my teeth and be a gay senorita. I'm going to have a *good* time."

I was having a good time just thinking about it. The weeks that followed seem to fly by. I had so much to do. For one thing I was really trying to concentrate on my Spanish. I hung on Mr. Hinson's every word during class and went through the halls muttering distractedly, *"¿Como está usted?"* I wished I had years of Spanish behind me instead of just weeks. Also, I was constantly practicing taking pictures with Dad's complicated single lens reflex camera. It had been clear to me from the start that my fuzzy pocket camera pictures wouldn't do for illustrating my book, so I had to borrow Dad's and master the technicalities of shutter speed and aperture. At the same time I was busy assembling lots of neat little traveler's helpers, things like drip-dry hangers that blew up like balloons and then deflated for packing, a clothesline with suction cups at each end, and a lead-lined pouch for carrying film safely through airport X-ray machines. It wasn't just that I thought I would need all those gadgets. I loved them for their own sakes. I love accumulating items labeled Travel Soap, Travel Hangers and Travel Clothesline. The very word *travel* gave me a thrill.

Unfortunately, when the time came to actually put my clothes in my suitcase, it began to look as if there would be no room for any of my gadgets. There wasn't even enough room for all my clothes.

I took out my faithful friend, *Traveling on a Shoestring*, and consulted it.

"Having trouble fitting everything in?" it said. "Try these methods." I was certainly having trouble fitting everything in, so I turned the page and read on.

"The throw-away method. Pack only your oldest clothes. Instead of washing them, throw them away as you travel. This leaves room in your suitcase for the souvenirs you will accumulate."

Back in the days when I had been reading this passage in the book stacks it had seemed like a super idea to me. But now that I was faced with doing it in reality, I could see some flaws in the plan. How was I going to attract the attention of any world-famous artists or bullfighters if I was wearing those old torn jeans I painted the house in last summer? And what about the boys who were going to be on the trip with me? Did I want to be known among them as the girl in the drip-dry rags?

I read on. "The wash-and-wear method. Pick one basic color, perhaps navy blue, beige or black. A few simple nylon outfits in these colors will dry quickly, be crush proof, and can be livened up by a judicious selection of brightly colored scarves so you will be appropriately dressed for most occasions."

I was doubtful. Not only did I look terrible in all those basic colors, but *nylon*? And what exactly was I supposed to do with a scarf to liven up the outfit? Wave it in front of me and shout *"Olé"*? At any rate, I couldn't very well go out and buy a bunch of new clothes in some basic color. I needed all the money I could lay my hands on just to take the trip. My hot pink jeans might not be basic, but I already owned them, which was the important thing.

The phone rang in the kitchen and I ran in to get it. Since we had started packing, Rosemary and I were in constant communication.

"I've done it," Rosemary announced. "I've coordinated everything to jeans and beige pants so I only have to carry two pairs of shoes. But I still can't seem to fit in the instant coffee and the Mars bars and stuff. Can't you carry half?"

"No way," I said. "It's all I can do now to squeeze in my raincoat."

"You ought to carry half the coffee," said Rosemary. "You're going to be drinking it, too."

"Not me. I'm going to go native and drink the local stuff. Why don't you ask Lolita?"

"I have. She says her suitcase is already filled to the brim."

"Buck up, Rosemary," I said. "You'll make it through this ordeal somehow."

My original plan had been to work ahead on my school assignments and get them all made up before we left, but by the time my passport arrived in the mail, I was too excited to concentrate on mundane things like algebra and history. Making up my work would have to wait until I got home. All I wanted to do was gaze at my neat, navy blue passport with the golden eagle embossed on the front. On the first page was a small photo of me, recognizable, if slightly bug-eyed, and at the back were lots of empty visa pages, which customs officials were supposed to stamp. I promised myself that in future years when I was working for the Foreign Service or pursuing my career as a roving star reporter, I would fill up all those pages.

At last, Wednesday afternoon, the week before Thanksgiving, Mom and Dad and I drove with Rosemary and her parents over to the Raleigh-Durham airport to catch our flight to New York. Our tour group was supposed to meet at an air terminal up there for the flight to Spain.

As soon as we got to the airport, I snapped a picture of our plane from the big window overlooking the runway. I had been taking heaps of pictures lately on the theory that I needed to get in the habit of taking them automatically. After all, I knew I could always throw the clunkers away if I ended up with too many, but there would be no way, once we got back, for me to replace any pictures I had missed.

"Don't forget to check the light meter, Cassie," Dad said.

"Don't worry, Dad. It's second nature to me now."

"And don't drop it," he said in anguished tones.

"Don't worry, Dad. I've practiced with it so much it's like an extension of my eye. And I'm awfully careful with it. Honest."

"I'm sure you'll do fine," said Mom. "Don't forget to write us as soon as you get there."

Rosemary and I left our parents all teary eyed at the terminal and boarded the plane. I had never flown before and was relieved, when we took off, to learn that I was not one of those people who get airsick. In fact, I decided, watching the layer of fluffy clouds beneath us, I liked flying.

When we got off the plane in New York and found the terminal where we were supposed to meet our group, it turned out to be full of brightly colored molded plastic seats and milling hordes of people. Mr. Hinson was standing near the ticket counter with a list to check off members of our group as they arrived. Some of the kids from our school had flown up the night before, and kids from other schools were flying in from all points of the compass, so there was a lot of confusion trying to make sure everybody was accounted for.

"Please check in with me, all the people on the Hockley High tour," Mr. Hinson was shouting. "I need to mark your name off the list."

"I think we did the right thing to nail down our roommates," I murmured to Rosemary. "Will you get a look at those kids?"

A girl with kohl-rimmed eyes wearing an emerald green coat had just passed by me and was getting her name checked off the list.

Rosemary grabbed my arm. "But look over there," she said. "*He's* gorgeous!"

She was looking at a tall, square-jawed boy with black hair and blue eyes. He was good-looking if you went in for the skinny sort, but he looked bored, standing there in a trench coat like someone out of a detective novel. How could anybody be bored about to set off for Spain? I wondered.

I eyed a girl with spiked red hair and a world-weary look who was edging up to Mr. Hinson. "I think they're all a pretty degenerate-looking bunch," I said.

Rosemary followed my glance. "We probably ought to comb our own hair," she said, touching hers uneasily. "You know how important first impressions are."

"I don't see what difference first impressions make. We're stuck with each other for two weeks, like it or not. We'd better get over there and check in."

I pressed my way through the crowd toward Mr. Hinson. When I got up to him he checked my name off and said, "Cassie, there's a message for you. Your Uncle Frank wants you to call him before you leave."

Rosemary shot me a questioning look, but I couldn't imagine what Uncle Frank wanted to talk to me about. It was hard to believe he had changed his mind about buying my story. I only hoped it wasn't bad news from home.

I made my way to a nearby pay phone and called him. "Uncle Frank?" I said. "Did you want to talk to me?"

"Hiya, Cassie. Just want to wish my favorite niece bon voyage and all that."

"You sent a message for me just so you could wish me bon voyage?"

"Well, there is one other thing. It turns out there *is* a story I'd be willing to buy from you, if you can get it. Now listen carefully. You know Barbara Channing?"

"I've heard of her." I had at least seen her picture on the covers of magazines. She had been a star in the movies for years, and after some years of retirement had returned, draped in jewels, to star on television. I had never seen her smash hit program because, unfortunately, it invariably conflicted with my algebra homework.

"She's starting what looks to be a very messy custody battle with her soon-to-be-ex-husband," Uncle Frank said. "She married a doctor years ago, and they've got three kids, a teenage boy and twin girls, aged five. Nobody knows much about them because the doctor fellow's been a maniac about his privacy. No interviews at their house, no photos of the kids. Now that they're splitting, she's charging him with child abuse and wants all three kids, but the word is he's going to fight it tooth and nail with countercharges."

"That's very interesting," I said. "But my plane is leaving pretty soon. Could you just touch on what I have to do with all this?"

"I'm getting to it. Now Barbara is giving interviews right and left while her lawyers are moving for an injunction to protect the kids from the father and also for a temporary custody order so she can have the kids until a final custody judgment is made. The kids are with the father now, you see, and Barbara's out in Los Angeles planning to marry her leading man. What we want to do is an article from the husband's point of view. You know the sort of thing, faithful spouse, wronged husband, innocent children suffering. But the doctor's keeping mum and he's moved for a closed court custody proceeding, which makes it tough from our point of view. This is where you come in. I want an interview with that boy of hers, some nice quotes, the inside story. Does the good doctor really beat up on his kids or is this accusation just a cynical ploy of Barbara's to get custody? You follow me."

"What I don't follow is how I'm supposed to get an interview with this kid," I said cautiously. "I'm going out of the country for two weeks."

"That's just it!" crowed Uncle Frank. "The kid's going out of the country, too. Touring Spain. They're probably trying to keep him out of the way of the press."

"So where can I find him?"

"I just told you. He's touring Spain."

"You mean that's all you know?"

"Look, if I knew where the kid was, I'd send somebody like Doolittle or Blake. I know it's a long shot, but just keep your eyes open. It'd be worth some money to me."

"How much?"

"How much do you need?"

"Four hundred."

"Okay, four hundred. Exclusive interview with the kid and I'll send you the cash. Easiest money you ever made."

Much as I would have liked to earn four hundred dollars and get out from under the thumb of my brother the extortionist, it didn't seem to me there was much chance of pulling off the interview Uncle Frank wanted. He had as much as admitted himself that it was hopeless. That's why he wasn't wasting the time of one of his own reporters. Of course, if I *could* pull it off, by some freak of fate, not only would I be four hundred bucks to the good, but I would be showing Uncle Frank that I was star reporter material. The idea had an appeal.

"What's the kid's name?" I said.

"Just a minute. I've got it right here. Wait a minute. Here it is. Hartington Warner Cameron III. Bear in mind he may be traveling under an assumed name."

With a name like that, I thought, who could blame him?

"I'm going to want proof that you've got the right guy," he went on. "Make him show you his passport. Take a picture of it and hand it in with your story."

"But you're acting as if I'm going to get the story, Uncle Frank. I don't think I can. Spain's big—it's probably crawling with tourists, and I've got to stay with my own group."

"Don't go telling me that," he said. "France is big, too, and when Velda and I did the Loire Valley we kept running into the same tourists over and over again. Everybody that goes over there hits the usual six attractions. I think you've got a chance. If you find the kid, just call the *Vision* office in Madrid. They'll send a runner to wherever you are to get the story. Or call me direct."

"I'll do what I can."

"Attagirl. It may come off, you never can tell. I hate to tell you how many times pure dumb luck has won the game."

"I'll do my best, Uncle Frank. I'd better go now. I need to look for a friend." I hadn't spotted Lolita yet and was getting a bit concerned.

"Don't be an idiot, Cassie. Your plane doesn't leave for an hour. What are you going to do? Sit around and stare at your ticket? Now listen closely, and you'd better write this down. Your Aunt Velda wants you to bring her back a Lladro figurine. Spelled l-l-a-d-r-o. Pronounced yah-droh. She wants it to be eight inches high. She want it to have flowers on it. And she does not want a bisque finish. She wants the shiny finish. You can get them anywhere over there. Be sure and have them pack it in excelsior so the thing doesn't get smashed. I'll reimburse you when you get back."

"Anything else?"

"No, I think that's all. Have fun."

I hung up and went to find Rosemary. "It was my Uncle Frank," I said. "The one that's the managing editor of *Vision*."

"You're so lucky to have a glamorous uncle like that," sighed Rosemary.

"Yeah, real lucky. You haven't seen Lolita yet, have you?"

"Nope, but you know how little she is. We've probably just overlooked her."

Just then the tall boy with blue eyes stepped up to give Mr. Hinson his name and we saw Lolita, who had been standing behind him. She grinned and waved at us.

"Good grief," breathed Rosemary. "Look at her suitcase!"

"It probably belongs to the tall guy."

"Oh, no, it doesn't."

Sure enough, as soon as Mr. Hinson had checked Lolita's name off the list, she grabbed the handle of the huge suitcase and began gliding it in our direction. I saw that it had wheels attached. A lucky thing, since it probably weighed more than she did.

"You're telling me you didn't have enough room for a few Mars bars in that monster?" said Rosemary indignantly.

"Sorry," said Lolita. "It was stuffed. I had to get my dad to sit on it, as it was."

Mr. Hinson had succeeded in checking off all the kids but one and he was calling out that name. "Harry Camden?" he called. "Has anyone heard from Harry Camden?"

The minutes passed and we all checked our luggage, but there was still no sign of the missing Harry Camden. I was glad it wasn't me that was in danger of missing the connection from New York to Madrid. I would have died.

We were actually lining up for boarding when Harry Camden came running up. He was dressed for comfort in old jeans, sneakers and a loose shirt with the sleeves rolled up, and he had a flight bag slung over one shoulder. After he got his name checked off Mr. Hinson's list, he came back and got in the line behind us, smiling at us uncertainly, as if he were a little embarrassed to have been so conspicuous. He had straight, very blond hair and eyes that crinkled at the corners when he smiled.

"Fella, you almost missed the plane," said Lolita. "Where's your suitcase?"

He smoothed his hair with one hand and said shyly, "I checked it on through to Madrid from home. Seemed easier."

"We should have done that, too!" said Lolita. "When we get to be world travelers we'll know how to do all that stuff, won't we, girls?"

Another boy came up and socked Harry on the arm. "Hey, Harry, you old fraud, you made it after all. Too bad."

"My friend, Mike, ladies," said Harry.

"I'm Lolita and this is Rosemary and Cassie. We're all rooming together," she said.

"Mike and I are rooming together, too."

Mike was sort of small and slender like Harry but with brown hair. Neither of them was glamorous looking like the blue-eyed boy in the trench coat, but they seemed nice. Maybe not everybody on this tour was degenerate, after all, I thought.

At that point, the line started to move and we filed through the flexible tunnel that led to our plane. As we went in, flight attendants were lined up on either side, like an honor guard, wishing us good evening. When Lolita and Rosemary and I found our seats and got settled, I read the safety instructions carefully, particularly the stuff about life rafts, since we were going over the ocean. I also fastened my seat belt. "I wish I were outgoing the way you are, Lolita," I said. "I can never think of anything to say when I meet strange boys."

"Child, I gotta make friends with some big strong boys fast. You don't think I want to carry that suitcase all over Spain, do you?"

It was dark now and the airport runway lights winked at us as the plane moved down the airstrip. After a good deal of taxiing and some distant-sounding roaring of the engines, we at last rose above the lights and left them behind. We were airborne and on our way. This was it. The butterflies in my stomach were fluttering so madly that I almost felt sick.

The blue-eyed boy in the trench coat was making his way down the aisle. As he passed us, Lolita called to him, "Excuse me, but have you found out when they're going to serve dinner around here?"

He steadied himself with an arm on my seat, and when he leaned over so we could hear him better, I got a smashing view of his clear blue eyes. "I just asked them that," he said. "After they finish serving all the drinks. Probably around nine."

His eyes mesmerized me. I tried to think of something intelligent to say but only managed to murmur something unintelligible.

After he moved on toward his own seat, somewhere in the rear of the plane, Rosemary grabbed my arm. "Those eyes. Aren't they to die for?"

"Nice," I agreed.

"Nice? All you can say is nice?"

"I like brown eyes better," said Lolita. It was a known fact that Lolita was inseparable from her basketball player boyfriend, Curtis. When it came to new boys, she was only interested in their suitcase-carrying capabilities.

I took out my black satin eye shades, which were among the traveler's aides I had been gathering together for weeks, and slipped them on. "The important thing now is to get some sleep," I said. "That's the way to avoid jet lag."

"Listen to her," said Lolita. "We're setting off on our big adventure and the girl is talking about sleep."

My eyes snapped wide open. She was right. I wasn't going to sleep. I was on my way to Spain!

Chapter Three

The next morning when the flight attendants started wheeling orange juice and Danishes down the aisle, my stomach reminded me that it was 2:00 a.m. Eastern Standard Time and a ridiculous time for breakfast, but the pilot was announcing over the speaker that it was eight o'clock and a beautiful sunny morning in Madrid where the temperature on the ground was twenty degrees. We would be landing in thirty minutes.

As I peeled the aluminum seal off my bottle of orange juice, I noticed that the tall boy was walking up the aisle again. I supposed that with his long legs the airline seats were pretty confining so he preferred to get up and walk around. I was trying to think of what I would say to him if I ever got the chance, when suddenly the plane bucked and he fell against me. Orange juice splattered everywhere and my empty coffee cup landed in Lolita's lap.

"Goodness!" she exclaimed.

"Excuse me," he said.

"Oh, that's all right," I said, blotting the orange juice off my sweater as best I could with my napkin. Lolita handed me her napkin and I took it gratefully.

The voice on the loudspeaker announced, "The captain has turned on the Fasten Seat Belt signs. Will all passengers please return to their seats and fasten their seat belts."

The boy slid into the empty seat across the aisle from us and buckled up. I looked anxiously out the window. "You don't think this means trouble, do you?" I said. "I'd hate to be killed in a plane crash just before I got there."

"Just a little air turbulence," said the boy. "Doesn't mean anything. I'm sorry about falling on you. Do you want my handkerchief?"

I was still swabbing at the orange juice splatters with my crumpled napkin. I didn't really need his handkerchief, but I reflected that I shouldn't let that stop me from making his acquaintance. "Thank you," I said, taking it from him. "You're with our group, aren't you? I'm Cassie, and these are my friends Lolita and Rosemary."

Rosemary had the disadvantage of being far over in the window seat, but she smiled her most charming smile.

"We're all going to be roommates," Lolita explained. "Do you have your roommates fixed up?"

"I just drew some names out of the hat," said the boy. He fished a slip of paper out of his hip pocket, put on some black rimmed glasses and read aloud, "Harry Camden and Mike Harper. Do you know them?"

"We've met them," said Lolita. "They're nice."

I admired the boy for being willing to put on his glasses. If I had blue eyes like that, nothing could have induced me to cover them up. I decided he must be very secure.

"What's your name?" asked Lolita.

"Trey. Everybody calls me Trey." He glanced up the aisle and said, "Maybe I'd better get back to my seat. We'll be coming down pretty soon, and I've got to get my things together."

After he'd left, Rosemary sat back in her seat and sighed. "Isn't he gorgeous?"

"Could stand to put on a little weight," I said.

A little later, the plane's wheels bumped on the runway. Soon we stepped out the door of the plane and into the thin, cold morning light of Spain. I pulled my coat tighter around me and tied a scarf over my head to keep my ears warm. Then, casting a quick glance around me to make sure no one was paying attention to me, I reached down and touched my fingers to the ground. Now that I had actually touched European dirt, I felt more sophisticated already.

The passport checkpoint and luggage claim area that we filed into was unheated and was decorated in a very understated way with a simple coat of khaki paint. When my turn came I handed the uniformed man my passport and murmured to him, "Is there a ladies' room near here?"

He looked at me blankly and I realized with a sinking feeling that I was in a country where people did not speak English. This could be a problem.

Harry came up beside me, the flight bag slung over his shoulder and said, "*¿Donde está el lavabo, por favor?*"

The official jerked a thumb to his right. Blushing hotly, I scurried off towards the ladies' room. I was anxious to get back before the group finished going through the passport line. It had struck me forcibly that it wouldn't do to get left behind in a country where the only word I could think of in moments of stress was *olé*.

When I got back, kids were standing by the luggage carousel picking up their suitcases. Lolita's monster bag had already been hoisted by Harry, who was carrying it along with his own. "So sweet of you," she said, beaming up at him.

We all rode on the airport bus into town. I was fascinated by the genuine foreigners we were driving past, all of them looking as if they could burst into a torrent of Spanish at the slightest provocation. I took lots of pictures. I snapped some men wearing berets, I snapped a handsome black-haired boy on a motorcycle as he zoomed past our bus with a roar, I snapped a pair of nuns walking into a building labeled Farmacia, then I increased the shutter speed and got a shot of a street corner vendor. Madrid did not look a bit like Hockley.

When we arrived at our hotel, I gave a deep sigh of pleasure. It was as foreign looking as the streets outside. The lobby had groups of middle-aged ladies in fur coats speaking Spanish, and next to the elevator stood a suit of armor. I snapped a picture of the suit of armor. When we found our way up to our fifth floor room, it had huge, dark pieces of gloomy furniture, the kind you might find in a hacienda. I flung open the shuttered window and found that it gave onto a balcony that overlooked an alley between buildings with red-tiled roofs. Across the way a woman was hanging laundry out the window on a pulley clothesline. "Look!" I breathed ecstatically. "Spanish laundry!"

"Close that window!" said Rosemary. "It's cold."

Before I did, I raised my camera to my eye and took a shot of the laundry.

"That camera is going to get glued to your eye, if you don't watch it," said Rosemary. "Every time I look at you you're taking a picture."

"I have to take pictures. I need them for my book."

"I didn't bring a camera at all. I didn't want it to interfere with my enjoyment of the experience," she said. "You know, some people get so wrapped up in picture taking that they lose touch with reality."

Rosemary could be very annoying, but, although I didn't realize it then, events were later to prove that she had a point.

Lolita was already busy unpacking. "If we're going to be here four days," she said, "we might as well make ourselves at home." Out of the big suitcase, she took six pairs of shoes, an iron, her blow dryer and a larger-than-life-size picture of Curtis in a gold frame. The next things to surface were a popcorn popper and a high school yearbook.

"You brought your yearbook?" I said.

"It's the little touches that make a person feel at home," she said.

"I wonder who's next door," said Rosemary. She tapped cautiously on the wall. "Yoo-hoo! Anybody over there speak English?"

"Sí, señorita," replied a muffled voice with a flat American accent.

"Let's go over and see who it is," I said. "Our balcony is right next to theirs. I'll bet I could just step over to their room."

"Don't do it," warned Rosemary. "We're five floors up."

Lolita peered briefly out the shutters, then closed them tight. "Room with view of alley. I hate to say it, girls, but I've stayed in better hotels."

I had never stayed in any hotels before, but this one seemed great to me. I hadn't gotten over the thrill of the armor next to the elevator yet. Rosemary was consulting our printed itinerary. "Ten o'clock lecture on Spanish art. Remainder of day at leisure," she read.

"First, I write to my Curtis," Lolita announced. "Then I sleep. I'm bushed."

I was bushed, too, but I figured I had better spend my free time out on the streets of Madrid looking for that Lladro figurine for Aunt Velda. It stood to reason that a big city like Madrid would have more of that kind of thing than some of the smaller towns we would be visiting later.

Just then there was a tapping at the shutters. Lolita and Rosemary and I all jumped a mile and grabbed at each other, remembering suddenly that we were in a foreign country.

"Who is it?" I called.

"American crazy people," replied the voice outside the shutters. "Let us in. It's cold out here."

I unfastened the shutters and Harry, Mike and Trey stepped one by one into our room.

"Have you folks figured out how to work the shower yet?" said Trey.

We all trooped into the bathroom to take a look at the thing. It was Lolita who quickly figured out how it worked. Meanwhile, I looked curiously at the extra plumbing, an odd knee-high, oval basin with faucets.

"It's a bidet," said Harry, following my look. "Great for icing champagne."

I was not keen to have European plumbing explained to me by Harry, so I made a prompt exit from the bathroom. A second later they all came out.

"I'm going to go get a shower," said Trey. He climbed back over the balcony to his own room and a moment later we heard the sound of running water next door. Mike lingered a bit longer, but soon shot us a shy look, mumbled something about writing postcards and disappeared out the shutters.

"I hope nobody likes to sing in the shower," said Lolita in foreboding tones. "These wall are thin."

"You girls don't happen to have any food do you?" said Harry. "Turns out there's no lunch until two o'clock. They eat at strange times over here."

Rosemary produced her Mars bars, and Lolita plugged in the popcorn popper. She had also remembered to bring a European circuit adapter and packets of prebuttered popcorn. I wasn't surprised. At that point, I had seen so many things come out of her suitcase that I wouldn't have been surprised if the next thing out was an easy chair.

Harry was soon stuffing handfuls of popcorn into his mouth.

"If lunch is at two, what time is supper?" I asked.

"Ten o'clock," Harry said.

"P.m.?" I said, aghast. "You mean ten o'clock at night?"

"People in Madrid eat late," said Harry. "I've already asked."

"Pass the popcorn," I said. Thinking of the hungry hours ahead, I began to wish I had packed a few Mars bars myself. "I've got to buy a porcelain figure for my aunt. Does anybody have any ideas about where I could get one?"

"Piece of cake," said Harry, licking the salt off his fingers. He pulled a map out of his hip pocket and spread it out on the table. "We're here," he said, making an *X* on a main street labeled Gran Via. "All you have to do is walk outside, turn right, and after six or seven blocks, you'll run right into one of the biggest department stores in Madrid."

Looking over his shoulder, I could see that a green flag on the map marked a store called Galerías España. Not coincidentally, I noticed, the map had been published by Galerías España.

"Where did you get that map?" I asked.

"Down in the lobby. I need to go out and pick up a few things myself. I packed in kind of a hurry." He smiled at me guilelessly. I noticed for the first time that his broad forehead under his straight blond hair proclaimed an impossibly sweet innocence. Nobody could be that innocent. On top of that, it was beginning to be evident to me that Harry was going to be one of those tiresome people who know everything. "I'm going to go right after the lecture," he said. "Want to come with me?"

"I'm not sure when I'll be going," I said. "I may want to get a cup of hot chocolate or something first."

"I might want to get some hot chocolate, too," he said.

"On the other hand, I might take a nap," I said.

"Oh, okay," he said, taking the rejection calmly.

Soon he departed through the shutters, still beaming innocence. "Thanks for the popcorn, Lolita," he said. "See you all at the lecture."

After he had left, Lolita said, "I don't know why you aren't nicer to that boy, Cassie. He's sweet about carrying suitcases."

"But I don't have to be sweet to him. I can carry my own suitcase. I don't want him always explaining things to me and telling me how to say it in Spanish and finding the way for me. It would be like being on a leash, for pete's sake. I want to see the world on my own."

I showed an alarming tendency to fall asleep during the ten o'clock art lecture. I decided I had better hurry up and get my errand done so I could sack out. As soon as we were released from the lecture, I cast a quick glance around to make sure there was no sign of Harry and hurried to the lobby. The first thing on my mind was to get a postcard off to Mom and Dad. I knew I could get postcards just about anyplace, but the only place I had seen *free* postcards was at the hotel and I was, after all, on a strict budget. From the display on the hotel's desk, I chose a postcard of the hotel dining room and sat down in one of the uncomfortable high-backed red chairs to write a quick note. "Dear Mom and Dad," I wrote. "Guess what! There is actually a suit of armor in the lobby of our hotel. Also we had a lecture on art this morning that was extremely educational. Tomorrow the Prado museum. Love, Cassie."

It was not great literature, but it would do. I hoped I could find some stamps to mail it with while I was out looking for the porcelain figurine. I tucked it in my purse, and checking once more to make sure there was no sign of Harry, I pulled on my coat and stepped outside onto the main street in front of the hotel. It was full of elegant shoppers and did not seem at all intimidating. I felt a moment of thrill. I was on my own in Madrid! I carefully checked the sign on the corner to make sure the street we were on really was named Gran Via, just in case Harry had got it all wrong. Then I headed in the direction of the department store. Making my way through the crowds on the sidewalk, I passed movie theaters, travel agencies, shops and a tempting pastry shop.

At last I saw, looming before me, a skyscraper that had Galerías España emblazoned across it. On the outside of the building a green-spangled outline of a Christmas tree at least four stories tall showed that the store was already gearing up for the holiday season. I pushed my way in through the heavy glass doors into the store and looked curiously around me. To my left was a big souvenir section with dolls dressed in green and yellow flamenco dresses and others in the tight black clothes of the matador. I was glad to see that tourists had obviously passed this way before. That meant the people here would know what to do about traveler's checks. They might even speak English. I went past a perfume counter and studied a store directory near the elevator with intense interest. Unfortunately, it was in Spanish and few of the words had been in the first four chapters of my Spanish book.

I turned to the clerk at the glove counter. "Do you speak English?" I asked.

She smiled at me. *"Español,"* she said.

That was not encouraging, but I persevered. "Lladro?" I inquired.

She nodded with comprehension and, stepping out from behind the counter, pointed overhead. I saw then that a mezzanine formed a half floor overlooking the ground floor. Presumably the porcelain was up there. *"Gracias,"* I said. Feeling pleased that I had just uttered my first Spanish word to a Spanish-speaking person, I made my way to the elevator.

Unfortunately, the elevator, instead of having numbers for floors the way sensible elevators do, had mys-

terious letters like *G* and *A*, which presumably stood for
even more mysterious Spanish words. I was at a loss
until a stout matron got in with me and pushed a button that took us up to the mezzanine.

As soon as I stepped out of the elevator, I knew I was
in the right place. The mezzanine was full of porcelain
figurines—tall shepherds playing guitars, dancing ladies, brightly colored birds, and along the wall in glass
cases, the most expensive porcelain was displayed with
a prettily crafted sign that said simply, Lladro.

I quickly located a figurine of a little girl carrying a
basket of flowers. It met all Aunt Velda's require-
ments. It was shiny, it was eight inches tall and it had
lots of flowers. A salesclerk appeared magically at my
side, and I indicated which one I wanted by pointing to
it. It was too bad that I didn't know the Spanish for
"Please wrap it in excelsior," but I figured that when I
got back to the room I could always stuff my underwear around it instead. She took it out of the case carefully and put it in a box with a little tissue paper around
it. Then she led me past several counters and over to a
cashier's booth where I could pay for it.

As I pulled out my traveler's checks I found myself
thinking that this business of being a world traveler was
pretty easy. Nothing to it, really. I signed the checks and
handed them over to the cashier. While she was getting
my change, I pulled out the postcard I had written my
parents and added the postcript, "Having a wonderful
time." Then I dropped it into the bag with the Lladro
figurine. Now I had two things I had to be careful of,
the Lladro piece as well as Dad's camera, but on the
whole I thought I was managing nicely.

The cashier handed me a handful of pesetas in paper
and coin. I hoped it was the right amount. I hadn't quite

learned to count pesetas yet. I curiously eyed the picture of King Juan Carlos on one of the heavy coins, then dropped the coins in my change purse and began looking around for the elevator. I realized that I had lost my bearings when the salesclerk led me to the cashier's booth.

Holding the bag with the figurine in it in a firm grip, I wandered past a display of children's gloves and caps and then past the men's mufflers. At that point I realized that I had to be going in the wrong direction because I was approaching the railing of the mezzanine. It might be nice, I thought, to look down and get an aerial view of all the perfume bottles and the flamenco dolls I had seen on the ground floor.

The wall around the edge of the mezzanine was waist high, and there was a brass railing running along the top of the wall. I carefully rested the bag with the Lladro figurine on the wall just inside the brass railing and peered below me. All at once, I was startled to hear loud popping sounds below me, like a string of firecrackers going off too close for comfort. I was thinking that it seemed like a bad idea to go throwing firecrackers around in a department store when I heard a scream. Then I saw that men with guns were standing just inside the big glass doors at the entrance, firing into the store.

When the huge glass chandelier on the ground floor went down with a crash and one of its crystal prisms rolled almost to the gunman's feet, I raised my camera to my eye and began snapping pictures. Through the camera lens I could see fire flaming from the barrels of their guns and an odd, frantic look on their faces as they braced against the guns' recoil. I'm not sure that it had dawned on me that I was watching a terrorist attack. In taking the pictures, I was acting mostly out of instinct. One of the tall flamenco dolls in the souvenir shop was hanging upside down from the shelf, I noticed, its head shattered, and I snapped a picture of that, too. Behind me I heard someone mutter, *"¡Madre Dios, llame a la policía!"* but I didn't turn around. I was intent on adjusting the aperture, bracketing my exposures so I could be sure my shots were properly lighted.

Suddenly I was rammed from the side with great force. As I hit the floor, my camera bounced up and banged me hard on the lip.

"Are you okay?" said a voice in my ear. I lifted my nose off the carpet against which it was pressed and saw Harry Camden on the floor next to me.

"My camera!" I wailed. "What if you broke it!" I groped for my purse, looped it over my shoulder and struggled to get up.

He held me down. "Shut up!" he whispered harshly. Just then I heard a crashing sound directly over my head. I glanced up and realized that my Lladro figurine, perched on the railing above me, had suffered a direct hit. Suddenly I felt cold.

"We're going to have to crawl to the elevator," Harry panted. "Follow me."

I was in no state of mind to argue. I crawled along behind him, hugging the ground closely, like a snake. We inched past a salesclerk who was huddled behind a counter holding a phone to her ear. *"¿Policía?"* she was whispering into the phone. We passed another woman who had covered her head with her coat and was huddled behind the glove counter.

When we reached the elevator, Harry reached up and pressed the Call button. An electric bolt of fear shot through my stomach. "What if it takes us down to the ground floor and then the doors open?'' I whispered. "We'd be in the middle of the shooting. We're taking a chance. Maybe we'd better not do this.''

"Taking a chance? You're somebody to talk about taking chances,'' he muttered wrathfully. "Do what you want, but I'm not staying here while they shoot up this place. I'm going to take the elevator down to the parking garage. I think I can get away from there.''

I could hear the claxon of a siren in the distance and nearer at hand the sound of gunfire falling into the deathly silence of the store where everyone huddled behind counters. I began to think Harry was right. I wanted to get out of there.

We crawled into the elevator and waited while its big doors closed. Then Harry pushed the bottom button, which was marked *G*. I prayed that he knew what he was doing and that the *G* stood for *garaje* and not, God forbid, "ground floor.'' The elevator sank with incredible slowness until I was sure we must have been at the ground floor. I felt sick and Harry looked very white in the face, but to our vast relief it kept on sinking.

When the doors opened, I felt like babbling in relief as all I saw was the echoing darkness of the parking garage. Harry held the doors open for me with one arm while I stepped out of the elevator. We looked around anxiously. The parking lot was full of deep shadows. "How do we get out of here?'' I whispered. Suddenly in the gloom I spotted what looked as if it must be a way out, a lighted sign that said Salida. We ran toward it, our running steps sounding loud in the echoing garage.

When we reached the door, I opened it a bit and looked out. To my relief I heard no more gunshots. In the distance I could hear a siren coming closer. The narrow street just outside the door seemed to be deserted except for a line of parked cars. We held hands and, glancing anxiously around, ran out into the street. Almost at once we turned down a cross street, hoping to put as much distance between us and the department store as possible. The grocery stores and shops we passed were closed, their windows shuttered as if they had been expecting trouble.

"Closed for midday siesta, I guess," Harry croaked. From the harsh sound of his voice, I could tell he wasn't as calm as he looked. He paused and, looking around uncertainly, pulled his map out of his jacket pocket and consulted it. Finally he said, "This way," and I followed him down an even narrower, even darker street where I saw a cabbage lying damply in the gutter.

Minutes later we turned again and came out once more on the broad avenue of Gran Via. Looking down the avenue in the direction of the store, I could see that the block was full of police cars. I shivered and looked away. My mouth felt dry. A taxi was parked near us, the driver leaning on it as he looked curiously in the direction of the police cars. Harry opened the taxi's door and got in. "Hotel Mayor," he told the driver. I had got in right behind him. I was glad to be able to sit down because my knees were showing an unfortunate tendency to buckle.

"You okay?" asked Harry as the taxi began to move.

"I guess so," I said shakily. I seemed to be undamaged except for a split lip and a bruise where my camera had smashed against my ribs.

Moments later the cab pulled up in front of our hotel. Harry paid the driver and followed me into the lobby. I knew that the Lladro figurine was somewhere back in that awful store, shattered in a thousand pieces, but it didn't bother me at all. I was only glad it wasn't me that was in a thousand pieces. My teeth had begun to chatter.

When we got up to my room, Rosemary and Lolita opened the door, looked at me wide-eyed and exclaimed, "What happened? What's wrong?"

"J-j-just a little terrorist attack," I said, giggling.

"Shock," said Harry. "Come on, Cassie. Let's get your feet up in some hot water."

I was happy to let them prop my feet up in a bidet full of hot water. Lolita brought me a blanket, and I pulled it close around me. "Oh," I said with a shudder, "I don't ever want to see another porcelain figurine. Or another chandelier."

I knew that was not a very clear statement, but I couldn't do any better. My teeth had started chattering again. When Harry gently took the camera on its strap from around my neck and took it into the room to put on the bureau, I realized that another thing I never wanted to see again was a camera. If it hadn't been for that awful camera, I told myself, I wouldn't have stood up there idiotically snapping away while the bullets were flying.

Harry leaned against the door frame of the bathroom. "We were in the store," he explained to Lolita and Rosemary, "and these guys came in and started shooting up the place. I didn't see how many of them there were."

"Three," I put in.

He shrugged. "Anyway, they were shooting in all directions, and Cassie and I barely got out of there. We had to crawl to the elevator and take it down to the parking garage and run from there."

"You saved my life, Harry," I said, pulling the blanket closer around my shoulders. "I would have stood up there taking pictures until I ran out of film if you hadn't tackled me."

"You could have been killed!" said Rosemary, her face white. "We'd better tell Mr. Hinson. He's going to want to call Cassie's parents. She'd better fly home right away."

"No!" I yelped. "I'm not going home!"

"Wouldn't you like to be back in your own bed," cooed Lolita, "with your own mommy to take care of you?"

"No! I don't want to go home. I just got here! You don't understand! This is my once-in-a-lifetime opportunity."

Harry smoothed his hair in a nervous gesture. "We might all go home," he said. "Mr. Hinson might want to call the whole trip off."

"Over my dead body!" I said. I realized too late that my phrasing was unfortunate. "Mr. Hinson doesn't even have to know about what happened," I said.

Lolita shivered. "Terrorism! I don't like it."

"An isolated incident," I said.

"He'll see it in the papers," said Harry.

"What papers? I didn't see any for sale in the hotel lobby," I said.

"You mean, not even tell Mr. Hinson how you and Harry almost got killed?" said Rosemary.

"Well, the news isn't going to make him any happier, is it?" I pointed out.

The quiet of the room was shattered by a loud knocking at the door. Rosemary, who was nearest the door, jumped a mile. "Wh-who is it?" she asked.

"I'm looking for Miss Cassie Wilkerson," said a man's voice in a strong Spanish accent. "I am from *La Vida*."

I pulled a blanket over my head. "I'm not here," I said. My desire for adventure had suddenly evaporated.

Chapter Four

I believe," the voice outside the door continued, "that Miss Wilkerson was taking photographs while the terrorist attack at Galerías España was taking place. *La Vida* is interested in buying the roll of film from her. Is Miss Wilkerson there now?"

"How did you find me?" I said suspiciously.

"Ah, Miss Wilkerson, you are in there, after all! The postcard in your shopping bag gave me both your name and the name of your hotel. I have the card with me now. If you will open the door I will give it to you."

"How do we know you're really from a newspaper?" said Rosemary.

"If you will kindly open the door I will be pleased to show you my identification," said the voice.

"I could sneak around by way of the balconies and check him out," murmured Harry.

A card was being slowly pushed under the door. "My identification, young ladies," said the voice.

Lolita picked it up and looked at it. "It says 'Luis Posada, *La Vida*,'" she said.

"I'm sorry, Mr. Posada," I called. "If the roll of film has any news value, I'm going to have to offer it first to my uncle, the managing editor of *Vision* in the United States."

The reporter on the other side of the door didn't actually say *"¡Caramba!"* but that was the flavor of the silence that followed.

"The man's going to need his press card, Lolita," I said. "Push it back to him." The water in the bidet was getting chilly, and I turned on the hot water faucet to warm it up some. She gingerly pushed the card back under the door.

"I will leave my name and number in case you change your mind," he called. "Goodbye, Miss Wilkerson. I heartily congratulate you on your so fortunate escape."

Before he left, he pushed something else under the door. Lolita picked it up, turned it over curiously then brought it to me. "This postcard's got problems," she said.

It was the postcard I had written to Mom and Dad. The reporter had penciled his name and number on the card, but that wasn't what caught my attention. What I noticed most was that there was a round hole through my last-minute P.S., "Having a wonderful time."

"Good Lord!" said Harry, looking over my shoulder, "It's a bullet hole."

I dropped the postcard, sank weakly back into my chair and pulled the blanket closer around me. "Some souvenir," I said.

"When are you going to tell this uncle of yours?" asked Harry.

"I guess I'd better do it now. Hand me a towel." I dried off my toes and limped my way to the telephone.

It took several minutes for the hotel operator to put through a call to New York. I hated to think what it was going to cost, but at last I heard Uncle Frank bark on the other end of the line, "Wilkerson here."

"Uncle Frank? It's me, Cassie."

"Cassie! Have you got hold of the Cameron kid?"

"Uh, not exactly. I think I've got a story you want, though. At least, the man from *La Vida* was very interested in it and offered to pay me for it."

"Cassie, what on earth are you talking about? Would you try to make sense for once?"

"Excuse me," I said, with dignity. "I have recently been the victim of a terrorist attack, and I guess I haven't quite recovered from the shock."

"What!"

"You see, I was in Galerías España buying that figurine for Aunt Velda and all of a sudden these guys opened fire and started shooting up the whole store. I've got it all on film. I must have taken twenty or thirty pictures."

There was a silence. Finally I said, "Uncle Frank, are you still there?"

"Of course, I'm still here," he said. "Are you okay?"

"Not a scratch," I said. "And I was very careful about the shutter speed and the aperture and focus, so I'm sure the pictures are good." I involuntarily shivered.

"You must have a screw loose, Cassie. Do you think I want my own niece massacred for the sake of a few lousy photographs? What were you doing taking twenty pictures? Why weren't you plastering yourself against the floor?"

"I did," I said, "eventually."

"What did Bob have to say about all this?"

"I haven't exactly mentioned it to the parents yet. I called you first thing because I figured you'd want the pictures right away. But if you're not interested, I'm sure *La Vida* would still like to buy them. Their reporter left his phone number."

"How much did he offer you?"

I unblushingly invented an offer on the spot. "Four hundred," I said. Four hundred was what I needed to get out of debt to Matt. I was sure the Spanish newspaper would have given me a decent amount, so I figured it wasn't exactly fibbing.

"Okay," he said, "I'll match their offer. Contributing to the delinquency of a minor, that's what it is. I hate to think what your father's going to say to me when he hears about it."

"Honestly, Uncle Frank, you're acting as if I staged the attack myself. It wasn't my fault." I wiggled my bare toes on the rug. "I just happened to be the right person in the right place. My reporting instincts took over from there. Oh, and I hate to tell you this, but the Lladro figurine went blotto, shattered in a thousand pieces. I hope this doesn't affect our agreement that you're going to reimburse me for it because that figurine wasn't cheap and you have to keep in mind that it wasn't my fault that it caught a bullet."

There was a sputter of static on the line. "Uncle Frank, are you still there?"

"I'm still here. I'm just covering my eyes. Would you do me the favor of staying out of the cross fire from now on?"

"Sure. And I'd like you to do me a little favor, too. Would you just not mention this to Mom and Dad? I don't want to worry them."

"You must be kidding. I can't keep something like that from your dad. The shock has affected your mind, kid."

"If Mom and Dad make me come right home," I pointed out, "it's goodbye to any chance of getting that other story you want."

"Now that I think of it," he said, "I'd naturally assume you would call home and tell them. No need for me to."

"Good. Oh, and I need to be reimbursed for this phone call. Overseas long distance is expensive."

"I'll take care of it. What hotel are you at? No, wait a minute, I see I've got a copy of your itinerary right here. Hotel Mayor, Gran Via, right? The Madrid office ought to have a runner over there in less than a half hour. Stay in your room until he gets to you. And Cassie?"

"Yes, sir?"

"Stay out of trouble."

"Yes, sir."

After I hung up I looked up to see the intent faces of Harry, Lolita and Rosemary, who had been listening to every word. "He wants the film," I said. "A runner will be coming by for it."

Harry picked the camera up off the bureau by its strap and handed it to me. "You'd better unload it, then," he said.

I drew back. "Maybe you could unload it for me," I said in a small voice.

He looked at me curiously, but sat down on a bed, deftly unloaded the camera and threw the roll of film to me.

"The sight of the camera makes me feel a little sick to my stomach," I explained.

"You poor thing!" said Lolita.

"Don't you feel unsteady on your feet at all, Harry?" I said.

"Now that you mention it, I do. But it might be that I'm about to faint from hunger."

Rosemary burrowed around in her suitcase and came up with another Mars bar. Harry promptly peeled back the wrapper and bit into it.

"Maybe I'm slow," he said, "but I don't see how you expect to sell those pictures, let your uncle splash them all over *Vision* and still expect to keep the news from your parents."

"They'll never guess I took the pictures," I said. "Who reads picture credits? Besides, the magazine won't even come out until next week. I'm not going to worry about it."

"You don't worry *enough*. That's your trouble," said Harry, glumly devouring the rest of the candy bar.

Rosemary began wringing her hands. I had never seen anybody actually do that before, and I watched her with great interest as she squeezed her long white fingers. "I don't know if we're doing the right thing to keep this from Mr. Hinson and from Cassie's folks," she said. "How will we explain it when later on they want to know why nobody told them about it?"

"Simple. You know how hard it is to get letters off when you're on vacation. We'll explain how we just didn't have the time to write and then it slipped our minds."

"Slipped our *minds*?" she said.

"Right. I'll get off the postcard that I wrote this morning. Then my parents won't expect to hear from me again for days, and by that time it'll seem believable that I've forgotten all about it."

I held up the postcard and watched the light from the window shining through the bullet hole. "I guess I'll have to rewrite this one," I said regretfully. "I'll pick up another one on the way down to lunch." Everyone's eyes were drawn to the bullet hole. "I used to wonder how people got those pictures of riots and wars and all," I said, "but now I see how it happens. You just concentrate so hard on what you're doing that you forget to be afraid."

A brisk knock sounded on the door. "Is Cassie Wilkerson here?" called an American voice. "I'm Ollie Britt from *Vision*."

Rosemary opened the door, and an overweight man in unpressed clothes stepped into the room. "Which one of you is Cassie?" he asked.

"I am," I said. "Are you the runner Uncle Frank sent?"

"Runner, hell," he said with a crooked grin. "I'm the bureau chief. Our office is right down the street."

He produced a press card and a passport for identification.

"Where's my money?" I asked.

He wrote me out a check.

"It's not that I don't trust you," I said. "But business is business."

"No problem. Where's the film? We want to get it on the four o'clock plane."

I handed it to him. "And if you could just settle my phone bill downstairs," I said. "Uncle Frank said you'd take care of it."

He tucked the film into a lead-lined pouch. "I'll take care of it," he said. He took out a notepad. "Now tell me all about what happened. Could you hear these guys saying anything? What language were they speaking? Just give me your impressions."

Suddenly the scene I had witnessed flashed before my eyes, and my teeth began to chatter again. Quite possibly, I thought, I was not the material intrepid reporters are made of. Harry took a look at my blue lips and said, "You can see Cassie's not up to talking about it. Let's skip it."

"Sure, sure, no problem," he said. Harry gently guided him out to the hall and closed the door behind him.

"Reporters," he said in a disgusted tone. "Lucky thing your uncle's an editor. With your connections in high places, he was afraid to push it."

"I thought he seemed nice," I said. I wished I had been up to giving an interview to the press, but this way my teeth had of chattering was a problem.

Pulling the blanket around me again, I gazed at the check with affection. "Golly, four hundred dollars. You don't know what this means to me. I can pay back my greedy brother and get out from under his thumb. I'm a free woman! On top of that, this check is a real milestone. It's my first payment for reporting. This could mark the beginning of a career."

"You plan a career as a combat-zone photographer?" said Harry.

"Naturally not. A combat photographer could end up getting killed and that would be a serious disadvantage in a career. But there are other glamorous things I could do. I wouldn't mind being a globe-trotting reporter who covered fast-breaking news from Stockholm to Sorento. That way I could live in Europe all the time."

"I don't know if I'd like that," said Lolita. "This is a nice place to visit, but I don't think I'd want to live here. For one thing, they've got these terrorist attacks, and for another, Curtis told me they don't even play basketball."

"Could you all please stick to the subject?" said Rosemary. "I say we should tell Mr. Hinson what's happened. I just don't like keeping all this from him."

"Rosemary, just forget about it," I said. "You don't know anything about what happened."

"But you told me what happened."

"That's hearsay. It doesn't count. For you, this is just another sunny day in Spain. No worries. No cares. Wouldn't you say it's about time for us to get some lunch around here?"

"I hope so," said Harry, "I'm starving. I'd better get on back to the room. The guys are going to start wondering what's happened to me."

"You aren't going to tell them are you?" I asked anxiously.

"Nah. If we aren't going to tell Mr. H., the fewer people that know about it the better."

When Harry left, I suggested we go on downstairs to the dining room. Rosemary was still muttering to herself as we descended the stairs from the hotel lobby to the restaurant. "I don't like it," she kept saying. Luckily when the waiter showed up at our table, she shut up and bent to study her menu. "Oh, good, here's an English translation," she said. "It turns out that *hambur-*

guesa means hamburger. I'd better remember that. I have a feeling it's going to come in handy. And it looks as if they've got apple pie, too.''

I was doing my best to control my impulse to jump up and check behind the pillars and potted plants to make sure no gunmen were lurking there. I felt pretty edgy, and though I was ashamed to admit it, a hamburger sounded pretty good to me, too. Between jet lag and being attacked by gunmen, I didn't think this was really the day for me to try something new like garlic soup or milk curd pudding.

"Better not let Mr. Hinson catch us reading the English menu," said Lolita's voice, coming from behind the huge menu.

"I just hope that's all he catches us at," muttered Rosemary darkly.

The hamburgers turned out to be different but good. Dessert didn't go so smoothly.

"How can they call this apple pie?" said Rosemary. She looked in disgust at the wedge before her, a single piecrust filled with custard and topped by a few thin slices of apple.

"Looks like a sort of custard tart," I said.

"I *hate* custard," said Rosemary.

"I'll take it," said Lolita, "and you can have my assorted pastries when they get here."

Unfortunately Lolita's assorted pastries turned out to be assorted custard pastries. For that matter, the "cookies" I ordered were custard filled, too.

"Who ever heard of custard cookies?" wailed Rosemary.

I opened my pocket guide to Spain and turned to the Dessert heading. "The national dessert of Spain is flan," I read.

"Maybe we should have gotten flan," said Rosemary. "What is it?"

"Custard," I said. "Do you think it's the only dessert they know how to make?"

The one advantage of the excess of custard, from my point of view, was that it stopped Rosemary from harping on the question of whether we should tell Mr. Hinson about what had happened. She didn't say another word about it until we got back to the room and started to bed down for an afternoon nap.

"What do you guys make of Harry?" she said.

"What do you mean?" said Lolita, pulling hairpins out of her French twist.

"He acts awful sure of himself for such a little weed of a guy," said Rosemary.

"Watch it, Rosemary," said Lolita. "Being tall's not everything, you know."

"Besides, he's not a little weed of a guy," I said. "He may not be exactly tall, but..."

"Haven't you noticed that he's not as shy as he seems? And that boyish, innocent look of his is just a front. He looked so honest, I was sure he was going to back me up on this business of telling Mr. Hinson. Ha! Was I ever wrong! I thought I could count on you, too, Lolita," said Rosemary reproachfully. "I thought you were a responsible person."

"I just feel like it's none of our business," said Lolita. "If Cassie and Harry don't want to tell anybody about it, it's up to them. Besides I think Cassie's right. This thing's an isolated event. Why get everybody all stirred up and ruin the trip?"

"Aren't you going to tell me how you thought you could count on me, too, Rosemary?" I said.

"No," she said, pulling the covers up to her chin. "I always knew you were crazy."

Lolita reached over to her bedside table to put a last hairpin back in its little plastic case and knocked the case off onto the floor. I jumped a mile as the wire pins hit the floor and scattered. "Oh, drat," she said, sleepily snuggling deeper under the covers.

Pretty soon, Lolita and Rosemary were sound asleep while I stared at the ceiling. I felt very vulnerable, as if I had a layer of skin missing, and every time I closed my eyes I saw three gunmen firing at me. It was very possible, I thought, that I might never sleep again.

Chapter Five

The next morning, we all began piling on a bus to go to the Prado museum. I looked around me as I got on, but there was no sign yet of Harry and his roommates. Mrs. Hinson was sitting in the seat behind the driver, knitting a sweater. Lolita settled into a window seat and stowed her guidebooks, her diary, her pocketbook, her camera and a small box of chocolate candy at her feet. Next she produced a small pillow to tuck behind her head and a cashmere lap rug in case of drafts.

"You think you've got everything you need?" I asked.

"So I believe in comfort," she said. "Is it a crime?" On the sidewalk outside the bus, a toddler wrapped up in many layers of sweater and coat stared up at her until his mother jerked him along. "Poor little thing," she said. "He's never seen a black person before. I wish I could explain it to him."

"I wonder where Harry is," I said, sitting down beside her.

Just then I turned to see Harry mounting the bus steps behind Trey.

Harry sat down in the seat across the aisle from me, and as soon as he did I immediately felt safer. I supposed this probably had something to do with his saving my life.

"Over your jet lag yet?" he asked.

"I guess so. What about you?"

The bus's motor roared and we drove away. "I guess," he said. "I keep wanting to look behind the doors and under the beds, though."

"I know what you mean," I said.

Luckily, my nervousness did not affect my appetite for sight-seeing. I looked with fascination out the windows as we drove down the wide avenue of Gran Via and made a half circle around some statues and splendid fountains jetting silver spray into the sunshine.

"This is Plaza Cybeles, people," called Mr. Hinson.

"Goodness," I said, leaning over Lolita to get a better look. "What's that over there? It must be some kind of palace."

Lolita consulted her guidebook. "It's the post office," she said.

"It can't be," I said. "Let me see."

I consulted the guidebook, and sure enough, it seemed to be the post office. Well, at least now I knew where I could get stamps.

We turned down a busy tree-lined avenue decorated with red-and-yellow flags. "Notice the flag of Spain, people," called Mr. Hinson.

I could hear a band in the distance, and there were crowds of people on the sidewalks. Our bus stopped at a red light, and a large group of soldiers carrying musical instruments and wearing burgundy berets crossed the street. I was amazed that Mrs. Hinson could keep on placidly knitting. I had never seen anything this interesting in Hockley. I leaned forward and watched.

"Looks as if we just missed the parade," I heard Mr. Hinson telling Mrs. Hinson. "Maybe I ought to check the newspaper in the future so we don't miss out on any of these special events."

I hoped he wouldn't do that. I was sure it would be better if Mr. Hinson didn't see a newspaper for the next few days.

The bus pulled up in front of a vast stone building, and Mr. Hinson stood up in the aisle. "Now, people," he said, "instead of us taking the usual guided tour around the museum, I want you to put to work all the things you learned in your lecture yesterday. In this way, as you seek out the Goyas, and the Velázquezes and other masterpieces on your own you will be learning actively instead of passively. I will be standing by in case you have any questions. Does everyone have his or her lesson sheet?"

There was a considerable shuffling of lesson sheets. A few minutes later, we found ourselves in a dim hall with immensely high ceilings. Harry consulted his work sheet. "It looks as though all the important stuff is on the second floor," he said.

"You don't mind if I sort of tag along with you, do you?" I said, following him as he headed toward the stairs. "The thing is, I'm feeling kind of jittery. I hope I get over this pretty soon. I'm supposed to be writing a book about the trip. I need to be taking lots of pictures for it, and I haven't taken a single one since it happened."

"I guess it'll wear off soon," he said. "It's like being in a car accident or something. It takes you a little while to pull yourself together afterward."

When we got to the head of the stairs, he paused and surveyed the room before going on.

"No gunmen?" I said.

"Not so far," he said.

Neither of us was entirely joking.

We came upon Mr. Hinson in a room full of Goyas. "Notice the light and nervous brushstrokes," he was saying to a group of kids clustered around him. "Goya painted very quickly and put in long hours at his work. When it got too dark to paint, he stuck candles all around his hat brim and kept on working."

I went through the room looking at the pictures and decided I didn't much care for Goya's stuff. His people looked like dolls. They weren't solid and there was no life in their eyes. Maybe the problem was the hot candle wax dropping down his back. I was not sorry to trail after Harry when he left the long room filled with portraits.

The next room we came to had only one huge painting on the wall. I recognized it right away. It was *Las Meninas*, Velázquez's picture of a little Spanish princess and all her ladies in waiting. But it wasn't at all like the reproductions I had seen of it. The people in the picture were life-size and looked real, as if they might step out of the canvas any minute. The little princess in her heavy brocade skirt looked very pleased with herself, the ladies-in-waiting bent respectfully toward her, the dwarfs were teasing a dog in the foreground and a court official paused in a doorway, silhouetted against the light behind him. Standing at his easel, bearded and holding his brush, was Velázquez himself, looking more important than any of them, more important than the princess in her richly brocaded dress, or the court official in sober black, more important even than the king and queen whose faces were reflected in a mirror on the wall. "I created all this," he seemed to be saying. "I, the artist."

The light played over the brocades and tumbled in the windows and doors, holding the whole big, complicated picture together and making it one of the loveliest things I had ever seen.

We looked at it together in silence for a while, and finally Harry said, "Well, they do say it might be the best picture ever painted."

I swallowed. "I can see that." I was bothered somehow by the little princess. She stood in the middle of the picture, preening herself and so sure she was the heroine of the story that she wasn't even noticing what was going on around her. I had the strange and uncomfortable feeling that I was like her. I was in such a haze of happiness about finally getting to come to Europe that I hadn't been paying much attention to the other kids on the tour. What did I even know about what Harry was like, much less the girl with the kohl-lined eyes or the girl with the spiky red hair? My book probably wasn't going to be a great work of art, I knew, but if it were going to be decent at all, I needed to record what was going on around me, the way Velázquez had. I needed to know what the other kids were experiencing, what *they* thought of Spain. I looked at the picture and tried to feel that I was alert and observant the way Velázquez was.

"What's the matter?" said Harry. "I thought you liked the picture."

"It's reminding me that I've got to get to work on my book. I've got to find out about some of the other people on this tour, find out what they're up to, take some pictures."

"Well, that's one response to great art."

I could hear Mr. Hinson's voice approaching from the hall outside. He had fallen to lecturing. "You will notice that art in Spain during this time was supported chiefly by the court and by the church. Velázquez was a court painter."

Harry looked up. "Here they come," he said. Then he looked swiftly at me. "How'd you like to go to this restaurant where Hemingway used to eat?"

"Golly, I'd love to," I said. "But our meal tickets are only good at the hotel. Isn't it awfully expensive?"

"I'll treat you. I don't want to go by myself, and Mike is going to the flamenco show tonight."

Mr. Hinson led a crowd of students in to see *Las Meniñas*. "You'll notice the influence of Rubens, which I pointed out yesterday," he said.

"My feet hurt," said Rosemary.

After Velázquez, there were still rooms and rooms full of pictures to see. By the time we finished touring the museum, I was sure everybody's feet hurt. We filed outside to wait for our bus. Mr. Hinson counted heads and found that all were present, but there was no sign of the bus.

"I can't understand it," he said. "I wonder if the driver has had some mechanical difficulty."

I sat down at the base of a stone pillar to rest my feet and watch how everybody's nose was turning pink from the cold. Predictably, Lolita produced from her large handbag a warm knit cap and mittens. She then inhaled some steam from the paper cup she was holding.

She had somehow managed to find something hot to drink. Trust Lolita. "I love Spanish hot chocolate," she said. "It's so thick."

"Where did you get that?" I asked, thrusting my hands in my pockets with a shiver.

"There's a cafeteria in the basement."

I looked longingly toward the museum entrance but decided I'd better not chance it. The bus could show up any minute. "I wonder where Harry is," I said.

Then I spotted him with a group of other guys over by a stone wall. They were throwing a pair of red dice against the wall and muttering incantations of some sort. Just then the bus came into view and a cry of jubilation went up. Harry's dice game quickly broke up and we all lined up on the sidewalk, anxious to get into the warm bus. "What were you all doing back there?" I asked Harry.

He smoothed his straight hair with the palm of his hand. "I was teaching the guys how to shoot craps."

"Oh," I said. "Isn't that a kind of gambling?" I asked. "I mean, you play it for money, don't you?"

"In a manner of speaking."

"What does that mean?"

"It means yes," he said, looking embarrassed. "I mean, you play it for fun, really. The money is just incidental."

"So it's really a game of skill, then?" I asked. "I don't know anything about it."

"Well, maybe not skill exactly, but some people have a system," he said.

"A system? Do you have one?"

"Sort of," he said. "I never play standing next to somebody on crutches or somebody with freckles."

"That sounds like superstition to me," I said severely. I climbed up onto the bus. It was lovely to feel the warm air billowing around me and whooshing up under my skirt as I went up the steps. Harry followed close behind me.

"Who's to say what's superstition?" he asked. "You've heard of gravity and magnetism, haven't you? Who's to say that there aren't some forces that pull on the dice?"

"Freckles? Crutches? You honestly think they have influence on the dice?"

"Naturally. Of course, I talk to the dice, too. You know, I sort of plead with them."

"It doesn't seem to me that it's very likely to work," I said, sitting down.

"Oh, I don't know." He took the seat across the aisle. "Haven't you ever heard about talking to plants to make them grow?"

I could just imagine what my grandmother, the staunch Methodist, would have thought of this conversation. But this was not the time for me to get preachy with Harry. I was trying to concentrate on being alert and observant, noticing the things that were going on around me. I took a memo pad out of my pocket and made a note to myself—"Crps gm Prado." "If you wouldn't mind, I'd like to be kept up to date," I said. "Let me know who wins the next game. I need lots of names and human interest stories for my book."

"Sure thing."

I turned to Lolita, notepad in hand. "Lolita, what would you say is the most meaningful thing you saw at the Prado?"

"The hot chocolate," she said, taking a last sip from her paper cup.

Rosemary was just behind us and I turned next to her. "What about you, Rosemary? What was the most meaningful thing you saw at the Prado?"

She slipped a foot out of her shoe and groaned. "The bus," she said.

The girl with the kohl-rimmed eyes was sitting next to Rosemary. I smiled warmly at her. "My name's Cassie," I said. "We haven't met yet, have we?"

"I'm Betty," she said, her eyes wide like a Kewpie doll's. "Our bus driver's kind of cute, isn't he?"

Our bus driver was forty if he was a day. I folded my notepad and put it away. I sensed there was not much point in asking Betty what she had found most meaningful about the Prado.

Rosemary was looking at our itinerary again. "Tomorrow it's the Royal Palace," she said.

"It has miles and miles of corridors and hundreds of rooms," said Lolita. "I remember reading that in my guidebook."

Rosemary groaned.

When we got back to our hotel room, Rosemary soaked her feet in the bidet. "This isn't at all what I had in mind," she said. "Where are the gay *señoritas*, the music, the bullfights?"

"There'll be plenty of gay *señoritas* at the flamenco show tonight," said Lolita. "But I don't think they have so many bullfights in the wintertime. I tell you what, Rosemary, you ought to try something new for dinner tonight. Don't just order the same old hamburger, get something new and exciting. That will cheer you up."

"I might as well," said Rosemary dolefully. "The hamburgers don't really taste like our hamburgers, anyway, not really. Maybe I'll try that garlic soup stuff.

What do you think, Cassie? Tonight let's go with the garlic soup. We'll live dangerously."

"Actually," I said, "Harry and I are going out to get dinner tonight."

"Going out without us? Going out to have fun?" said Rosemary.

"Hush, Rosemary," said Lolita. "It's a d-a-t-e."

Rosemary looked at me in astonishment. "Cassie, you aren't getting a thing about Harry, are you?"

"Well, since he saved my life, I'm naturally likely to notice that he has some good qualities."

"He's not your type," said Rosemary firmly.

"Rosemary, soak your head," said Lolita.

"I saw him over there throwing dice," said Rosemary. "He's not dependable."

"We share an interest in the great writer Hemingway," I said. "We are going to a restaurant where Hemingway used to hang out."

I was especially glad to be going out with Harry because the flamenco dancing was optional and I could not see my way clear to the extra thirty-five dollars it was going to cost.

"You two are both going to the flamenco thing tonight, aren't you?" I said. "I need somebody to take some pictures of it for me."

"Don't look at me," said Rosemary. "I didn't bring my camera."

"You can use mine," I said. I knew Dad wouldn't approve of letting Rosemary use his camera, but I was desperate. Here we were on day two of our trip, and I had only had a few shots of nuns and motorcycle riders. And even worse, if I were honest with myself, I had to admit I wasn't sure I would ever be able to take a photograph again. The problem was that some primitive part of my brain remembered how that camera had almost got me killed and every time I went near it my hands started to shake. If Rosemary was able to get some decent shots of the flamenco dancers, maybe I could let her take all the pictures for my book.

Rosemary looked at the camera distrustfully. "Forget it," she said. "I can't work one of those things."

I was afraid she was right. I knew from experience what a klutz Rosemary could be, so I turned expectantly toward Lolita. After all, she had shown all that mechanical aptitude with the bathroom shower.

She shook her head. "Honey, I can't work a camera like that. Now if you want me to take a few shots with my little pocket camera, I'll do that."

"But you just can't get the sharpness you need with those little cartridge-type cameras. Come on, Lolita. I can show you how to work it."

"No, thanks. I'd go crazy with all those little buttons, and chances are I'd mess the pictures up, anyway."

I started to argue with her, but remembering all the weeks I'd spent learning how to work the camera, I began to have the uncomfortable feeling she was right.

What was I going to do? Could I imagine my book illustrated with those clever line drawings of mine that had been so admired in the second grade? Could I imagine that the day would soon come that I would feel like taking pictures again? I couldn't imagine either one of those things. That was the problem.

I would figure out something, I told myself.

Harry had called the restaurant and learned that they opened at the revolutionarily early hour of eight-thirty, so I borrowed Lolita's warm hat, put on a sweater, a coat, a muffler and gloves and at eight I left with him to get dinner.

"It's not far," he said, consulting his map. "It's pretty close to Plaza Mayor, and that's only a few blocks from here. Let's walk."

We set off down Gran Via, and I was amazed to see that the shops were all lit up and the streets were very crowded with people. Everyone, from grandmothers to little children, had bundled up against the cold and come out to take a walk. Lots of people were nibbling on pastries, and there was a holiday atmosphere. A snack shop we passed was crowded with people buying custard-filled pastries.

"It's the *paseo!*" I exclaimed. I remembered now that I had read that in Spain everybody came out and took a walk in the evening, but I had imagined that the *paseo* was something people did in the summer. I never dreamed that the custom held even in the winter.

We turned off Gran Via and walked a block down a narrower street. Suddenly I heard music and the booming voice of someone singing over a loudspeaker. When we rounded the next corner, we met with crowds of parents and children bundled up in coats and caps. Down the street, a gigantic doll as tall as a building was singing songs. His mouth and his arm moved with slow mechanical precision. I could see now that he was holding the figure of a child in his giant hand and singing to it. Behind him was a castle outlined in lights. Harry put his hand around my waist so we wouldn't get separated, and we joined the crowd headed toward the giant. When we got closer, I could see a whole row of smaller animated figures moving in time to the music. A girl holding a wreath of flowers whirled round and round, and a fiberglass deer twitched his white tail. Behind them was a life-size nativity scene.

"It's a Christmas display!" I exclaimed. Parents were holding their children on their shoulders so they could see better. Strings of lights and small floodlights lit the scene.

Harry consulted his map. "Wonder what place this is," he said. "It's not on my map." He studied the map, then with a wry smile folded it and put it away. "Oh, I get it. My map is put out by Galerías España. We must be at a competing department store."

"This is a department store?" I said. I pulled my cap down over my ears. "Let's go," I said.

I didn't actually think that terrorists were lying in wait in every department store in Madrid. In fact, I didn't actually *think* anything. It was just that I felt like keeping away from department stores for the foreseeable future.

The music followed us down the street as we walked away past lighted shop windows full of dolls and toys, mittens and mufflers, and ruffled flamenco dresses with matching shoes. We walked for a number of blocks, but at last I could tell we were getting to the restaurant area near Plaza Mayor because the shop windows became smaller and were decorated with strings of garlic and with the carcasses of small pigs hung by their feet. I averted my eyes from the pig carcasses.

"Here we are," said Harry. "Le Botin."

A dark man in a white coat opened the door for us, and we stepped inside where it was warm and smelled of roast pork and garlic. Blue-and-white ceramic tiles gleamed against the dark wood of the walls of the room. Smiling, the waiter led us through a doorway that was an archway of brick and then up a wooden staircase that looked old and narrow enough to have belonged to a smuggler's hideaway.

He seated us at a small table near a window with diamond-shaped leaded panes, a style that had last been current back in the time of Queen Elizabeth and the buccaneers. I sat down and looked around me. "Don't you love this place? It's perfect! So old, so European! Look at those bare beam ceilings."

"Hmm," said Harry absentmindedly. He opened the menu. "What do you think you'll have?"

I opened my own menu and discovered there was no English translation. This discovery muted my enthusiasm for a moment. I was very hungry, and it was crucial that I get something that had some nourishment in it. Preferably something with vegetables. It seemed like a long time since I had seen a vegetable. I didn't want my first trip to Europe to be marred by an attack of scurvy.

"What's the Spanish for vegetables?" I asked.

"*Legumbre*, I think. Something like that."

I found something on the menu that mentioned *legumbres* and settled on that. Harry did the ordering, as there wasn't much point in my pretending my Spanish was up to it. After the waiter left, I leaned over the table and whispered, "I think this room is filled with Americans."

"What makes you think that?"

"Look around you at all these men in V-neck sweaters. I don't think Spanish people wear V-neck sweaters."

"Maybe you're right," said Harry, looking around. "I guess we're eating kind of early by Spanish standards."

"But so far we haven't seen any tourists that are our own age," I said thoughtfully.

"Most kids travel when school is out," he pointed out.

"I'm beginning to think Uncle Frank was right."

"Right about what?"

"Oh, this story he wanted me to get for him." I realized that I had probably said too much. The movie star's kid was going to be hard enough to run down without everybody running around talking about what I was up to. I began intently studying the little folder on the table about the history of the restaurant. "Did you realize that when the Pilgrims were planting corn in Massachusetts, this place was already an inn for sheep herders?" I said.

Harry shot me a curious look and filled my glass.

"This water doesn't look quite right," I said. "Do you think it's safe to drink?"

"It's wine and it's safe to drink as long as you don't overdo it," he said.

"They didn't ask you for your ID?" I breathed.

He smiled and his eyes crinkled at the corners. I suddenly realized that they might not even have ID cards in this country. Possibly the legal drinking age in Spain was ten, or something. I took a cautious sip. I wouldn't have called it *good* exactly, but I noticed that a sip or two sort of deadened the hunger pains. I realized I was going to have to learn the Spanish word for snack as soon as possible. The opportunities to eat regular meals in this country were far too far apart.

I kept sipping the wine, and by the time the food arrived, I had had enough that I wasn't feeling particularly hungry at all. I was also feeling warm all over.

"Better eat something," said Harry, shooting me a look.

"I can't wait," I said. "Look at these vegetables! Mushrooms and artichokes yet!" My mouth full, I said, "This is *indisputably* the best thing I have ever eaten. Perhaps you would care to share one of these utterly heavenly artichokes? Or some of these divine mushrooms?" Then I caught sight of his plate. "Yuck!" I said. "What's the matter with your shrimp?"

"They just cook them whole, I guess, that's all." He pulled off the head and antennae of a large shrimp and proceeded to take off the shell. After popping it in his mouth, he rinsed off his buttery fingers in a little bowl of water that had a lemon slice floating in it.

My head felt light and a bit larger than usual, and the world around me seemed shinier than usual, too. "I've always wanted to do this," I said, leaning my elbows on the table and supporting my chin in one hand. "All my life I've wanted to travel to Europe and sit in beautiful restaurants and soak up local color and eat artichokes. One of my basic ambitions is to eat snails. I would also like to ride on a camel."

Harry devoured another shrimp. "That ought to fit in okay with being a globe-trotting reporter."

"That's right," I said. "And I'm already on my way. I've already got paid for my first story. Four hundred dollars."

"Getting shot at is earning money the hard way, though."

"There is no easy way to earn money," I said grandly. "A person has to be alert to every opportunity. Uncle Frank wouldn't have paid me a penny for those pictures unless I had told him that Spanish magazine had made an offer. And if I hadn't sold Mr. Hinson on the idea of writing a book about this trip, I would still be sitting at home reading travel books instead of being here eating these utterly yummy mushrooms." I looked around me to make sure no one was listening. I hadn't really planned to tell Harry about my hopes of selling another story to Uncle Frank, but now that I felt all warm inside from the wine, I suddenly felt like confiding in him. "I have another idea for earning money, too," I whispered. "Uncle Frank has promised to pay me if I get this human interest story for him. Maybe deep down he has more respect for my reporting skills than I thought."

Harry refilled my glass. "I'll bet you'd be good at doing human interest stories," he said.

"Well, I hope so," I said, suddenly feeling doubtful. "At any rate, I'm going to give it a try. Since I've noticed that there don't seem to be many kids our age traveling around Spain this time of year. I feel a little more optimistic. Have you ever heard of Barbara Channing?"

Harry bent to pick up the napkin that had slid from his lap. "Yes, I've heard of her," he said.

"Uncle Frank is very keen to get the inside story on her divorce, for some reason. All I have to do is track down her son and induce him to tell all. He's supposed to be traveling in Spain right now, but probably under an assumed name."

"If he's not using his own name, how will you know when you find him?"

"Intuition. Also logic and the process of deduction. To tell you the truth, I haven't quite worked out the details yet. I've sort of had my hands full trying to do the research for this book on the trip that I'm writing." I looked glumly down at my casserole with its succulent bits of artichokes. "The fact is, I've run up against a significant snag. I think I've got camera phobia." Suddenly I remembered the deft way Harry had taken the film out of the camera yesterday. "Wait a minute," I said excitedly. "You know how to work a single lens reflex camera, don't you?"

"Yup."

"Maybe you'd like to take the pictures for me."

He took a sip of wine. "I guess I could do that. Do you think half of what you net on the book would be a fair price?"

"Two hundred dollars?" I said. "You'd want two hundred dollars for taking the pictures?"

"Well, the pictures are really going to be an important part of the book, aren't they?"

I realized that Harry had taken all too seriously my little speech about grabbing every opportunity to make money. I had been hoisted by my own petard.

"Of course maybe you could find someone to do it for less," he said.

"No, no," I said hastily. "Half of the net is fine." After all, I had already asked both Lolita and Rosemary and had no luck. It was possible that somebody else on the tour knew how to work an SLR camera, but it would take me a while to find him, and meanwhile days were whizzing by unrecorded on film. Time was running out on me. And having Harry do the pictures had its advantages. In my current state of shattered nerves, I seemed to feel as if I had to stay right near him, anyway. We might as well be working as a team.

I impulsively put my hand over his. "You know, Harry, I think you're nice, even if you do gamble."

I reached for the bottle, but Harry moved it down onto the floor. "Maybe we'd better lay off now," he said. "We don't want to end up with headaches tomorrow morning."

"Oh, does wine give people a headache?"

"It's been known to happen. Want some dessert?"

"I don't think so. It always seems to be custard, somehow."

Harry signaled the waiter, and he appeared at the table with the check. He seemed like such a nice waiter. I smiled at him warmly. *"Me gusta el pollo,"* I said. *"Es bueno."* It was amazing how I suddenly felt more fluent in Spanish. Words only dimly remembered suddenly started coming to me.

"Gracias," he said, looking pleased. "Would you like to see the kitchen?"

"Oh, yes, I mean *sí*!"

"Just follow me, if you please."

Harry guided me down the narrow steps behind the waiter. "Watch your step, Cassie. You don't want to land on your head."

"I'm fine," I said. "Perfectly fine."

We went down several flights of narrow steps and found ourselves in a shadowy little cellar complete with spiderwebs where kegs and racks of wine were stored on their sides. A cold breath of musty air hit me in the face, momentarily clearing my head.

"The wine cellar," said the waiter. "This way to the kitchen."

He led us next to a brick archway through which I could see the cook, his face pink from the heat, pulling something out of the oven on a long-handled shovel-like thing. The ancient oven was like a cave made of bricks and completely lined with glowing coals. Then I realized he was taking out one of those small pigs with their feet bound together. "Amazing," I said weakly. I managed to steady myself by holding on to Harry's arm.

I was still holding on to him when we went out on the street, which now was almost empty, and very cold. I could hear our footsteps on the sidewalk as we passed the shuttered shops. Harry hailed a passing cab and soon we were speeding through the silent streets back to the hotel.

Suddenly I felt very tired. I leaned my head against Harry's shoulder. "Wasn't that a wonderful restaurant?" I said sleepily. "Except for when I was thinking of those sweet little pigs I loved every minute of it."

"We better get you to bed," he said, patting my head.

When we got back to the hotel, Harry opened the door with my key and bid me good-night with a friendly pat on the shoulder. As soon as I stepped foot inside, I was met by the horrified face of Rosemary. Lolita didn't notice my entrance much, as she was stomping her heels on the floor and lifting her arms gracefully over her head and shouting, *"¡Olé!"*

I watched her appreciatively and clapped.

"Cassie Wilkerson!" said Rosemary. "You've been drinking!"

"Just a little wine," I said, humming a tune. I slipped out of my shoes and collapsed on my bed. Getting into a nightgown seemed like rather a lot of trouble. Maybe I would sleep in my clothes. Especially because whenever I closed my eyes the room seemed to be rotating slowly. Yes, on the whole it seemed safer to just stay put in bed.

"Look at that, Lolita!" said Rosemary. "That boy has been plying her with liquor!"

Lolita executed a tricky little movement with her feet, breathed another *"Olé"* and then paused to peer at me. "Cassie, are you okay?"

"Fine. I'm perfectly fine," I said.

"Her eyes look glassy," said Rosemary. "Maybe we better fix her some hot coffee."

"Not on your life," said Lolita. "Then we'll just have a wide-awake drunk on our hands."

"I am not drunk," I protested. "I'm only very happy. Though possibly I shouldn't have drunk that wine on an empty stomach. No doubt that is the difficulty."

Rosemary clutched her hands together tightly. "Maybe we'd better go get Mrs. Hinson. She'd know what to do."

I sat up suddenly. "Rosemary, if you say another word about telling the Hinsons anything I will scream. I promise you I will scream and it will be very embarrassing for us all."

"Maybe we can just let her sleep it off," said Lolita.

That was the last thing I remembered hearing before I sank into velvety blackness.

Chapter Six

The next morning when we toured the Royal Palace, my head hurt, my mouth felt like cotton and I completely understood the state of mind in which people run away to join the French Foreign Legion. I tried to remember everything I had said and done at dinner the night before so I would know exactly how embarrassed I should be, but the effort of thinking only made my head hurt more. I vaguely recalled that I had been seized by the conviction that I could speak Spanish. That was bad enough.

Our group trailed behind our guide through vast halls as big as train terminals. Enormous chandeliers of crystal and gold hung from the ceiling, and I had the sensation of passing hundreds of gold cupids holding clocks.

"How many rooms did you say there were in this place?" Rosemary asked Lolita anxiously.

Lolita consulted her guidebook. "Two thousand eight hundred," she said.

"I hope that's counting broom closets," I said.

The guide overheard us and smiled. "Ah, but on the tour we only visit sixty-two of the rooms."

"Only sixty-two?" I said. "Well, that's a relief." Unfortunately a good many of the rooms were the size of train stations. I was not surprised to learn that the present king lived somewhere else. The Royal Palace wasn't exactly strong on coziness. It ran to ceilings covered with plump angels, sweeping staircases and gold-plated everything. Another time I might have been more interested in it, but just then all I cared about was getting a drink of water somehow.

The tour of the palace seemed to take forever, but at last it was over and our guide deposited our group just inside the entrance to wait for the bus. Most of the kids collapsed on a nearby staircase. I, however, managed to limp over past a postcard display to a bar where drinks were being sold. I looked carefully at the pictures of the drinks posted on the wall behind the bar. I was going to have to be very careful that I didn't end up with something deadly like an ounce of whiskey. Finally I spotted a picture of a glass full of an orange liquid. That seemed safe enough. I didn't think either wine or whiskey ever looked orange. I put my coins on the counter. *"Una naranja,"* I said to the bar man. He poured a canned drink over ice in a glass and put it on the counter before me.

"The hair of the dog?" said Harry.

I turned to see his innocent face beaming at me. "What did you say?" I asked.

He smoothed his hair. "Just a saying. Forget it. That looks good. What is it?"

I drank down a large swallow of my iced drink. "It's some kind of orange drink," I said. "I seem to be awfully thirsty."

Rosemary poked her head around the postcard stand and said, "The bus has come, Cassie. Hurry up!" Spotting Harry beside me, she took a moment to glare at him disapprovingly before rushing off.

I gulped down the rest of my drink, and Harry and I made our way back to the rest of group who were dragging themselves from reclining positions on the staircase. I realized that we were all beginning to look a little the worse for wear. Only Lolita remained immaculate in her neat French twist and her crisp clothes. This was probably because only Lolita had packed both her iron and her hair dryer. The other kids on the tour, who had looked degenerate at the airport in New York, looked even worse now in wrinkled clothes and hair that stuck out, yet I was already getting used to their faces. I could tell it wouldn't be long before the girl with kohl-lined eyes and the girl with the spiky red hair would look completely normal to me.

I could see Trey's tall figure up ahead of us climbing into the bus. Rosemary was with him, talking animatedly.

"What's this Trey person like?" I asked Harry.

"Thinks he's God's gift to girls," he said.

"No, I mean what is he like as a person? You've been rooming with him, so you must have some idea."

Harry shrugged. "He sort of keeps to himself."

Ah, I thought, a mystery man. Very interesting.

"He's kind of fussy," Harry went on. "Always dusting lint off his clothes, spends hours brushing and flossing his teeth, uses mouthwash. You know the type."

I preferred to think of Trey as a mystery man and re-fused to imagine him brushing his teeth. An interesting thought had occurred to me. I seemed to remember that a trey was what you called a playing card numbered three. If someone were named Hartington Warner Cameron III, wouldn't Trey be a likely nickname?

"Talking about roommates," said Harry, "what's Rosemary got against me? If looks could kill, I'd be dead meat."

"She doesn't trust you. She thinks you've been plying me with liquor."

"Not true. Don't you remember how I warned you not to drink too much of the stuff?"

That was true, he had. I also remembered that he had moved the bottle out of my reach. I remembered it too well. I felt embarrassed just thinking about it. "I guess I said some pretty silly things. I seem to remember speaking Spanish," I said.

"You were fine," said Harry, smiling at me. "Per-fectly fine."

We were the last people to mount the steps to the bus. There were only a few seats left at the back of the bus, so we went back there. Harry stretched his legs out and put his arm up on the seat behind me. He was certainly very close to me, and yet he wasn't quite putting his arm around me.

As the bus lurched to a stop outside our hotel, Mr. Hinson got to his feet. "Remember, people," he said, "we leave Madrid tomorrow morning. All suitcases must be out in the hall at seven-thirty. We leave at eight sharp."

There were groans all over the bus.

Rosemary, however, was unconcerned. When we got back to the room, she threw herself on the bed and sighed deeply. "Did you see how I was sitting with Trey?" she said. "He has a cocker spaniel, too. I knew we were going to have a lot in common."

Lolita cast a critical glance around her. "Girls, we'd better start packing. This place is a mess."

I could see what she meant. In the three days we had been in Madrid, we had bit by bit taken things out of our suitcases and now panty hose, socks, mittens, postcards, combs and sweaters were strewn all over the room in such confusion it looked as if a Goodwill Industries truck had overturned.

"Ain't no way we can pack tomorrow morning. Seven-thirty is awful early," Lolita pointed out.

Just exactly how early it was didn't hit me until we assembled with pallid faces the next morning in front of the bus, the first pale streaks of dawn coloring the sky. Mrs. Hinson was standing at the door of the bus swinging a plastic bag full of wet laundry and calling, "Who has lost his underwear? Would you please claim your underwear?" I shuddered and hunched my shoulders against the cold, glad that I wasn't missing any underwear. Harry appeared at my side. "If this is Wednesday it must be Salamanca," he said. His hair was still damp from his morning shower, and his ears were pink with cold.

"Is Salamanca really next?" I asked. Somehow in the rush to get packed the night before, Rosemary's copy of our itinerary had gotten misplaced.

"Well, Salamanca's where we finally get to rest our weary heads tonight, but first we see El Escorial and Segovia. At a dead run, I guess."

Our drive to El Escorial passed as if in a dream. Buses always make me feel sleepy even when I'm not tired. I was still half asleep when we toured El Escorial, where all the Spanish kings are buried.

I had regained consciousness and become more alert by the time we got to Segovia. I looked out the bus window and saw a castle perched on the point of a rocky cliff, its pointed capped towers silhouetted against the pale winter sky. I caught my breath. Here it was, a castle in Spain, just the way I had dreamed of it. Our bus made its precarious way up to the town through narrow streets and let us out right at its entrance.

We followed Mr. Hinson into the castle and through dimly lit rooms filled with armor and tapestries. The castle was rich with paintings and carved ceilings, but it had a curiously deserted air. Its heyday had come and gone. Now only guards and tourists paced its halls. Next we went up the winding stone staircase that led like a corkscrew to the castle's tower. The way was so narrow and dark that I had the sensation of climbing up a chimney. But at last we stepped out into sunlight and a spectacular view.

Trey squinted at the vista of the flat, dry countryside spread out far below us and said, "I guess you could see a rabbit five miles away from here, let alone an army."

"Oh, look!" said the girl with the kohl-rimmed eyes. "If you come over here you can see the town and the cathedral."

I followed her over to that side of the tower and got a good view of the dusty town with its orange-tiled roofs, the bell towers of churches standing among them like exclamation points.

It was odd to think that back when Ferdinand and Isabella built this castle it was the latest thing in defensive warfare, a sort of fifteenth-century version of the cruise missile.

Before we left the castle, I made a point of sneaking back to the throne room and sitting in one of the thrones where Ferdinand and Isabella had sat back in the old days. "Go to it, Columbus. Get out there and discover America," I said with a grand gesture.

Harry stuck his head in the door just then and grinned. "I thought this is where you'd be," he said. "Come on, everybody's getting on the bus."

I jumped up quickly and followed him out of the castle. When we dashed out the castle entrance, the bus's motor was already running, which made me nervous. "You don't think Mr. Hinson would really leave any of us, do you?" I said anxiously.

"Well, we'd probably have to be more than a little bit late for him to leave without us."

As we filed to the back of the bus to look for seats, the bus pulled away from the castle. Mr. and Mrs. Hinson were immersed in consulting timetables and didn't even seem to notice us getting on, but Rosemary scolded me as I passed her. "Where *were* you, Cassie?" she said. "One of these days you're going to get left."

"I just went back to look at a few things," I said guiltily.

Harry and I settled into our seats at the rear. "How did you guess where I was?" I asked him.

"I don't know. I just figured you'd be on the throne."

"You think I've got delusions of grandeur, that's it, isn't it?"

"Nah." He smiled. "I think you've got an imagination, that's all." Then he put his arm around me.

I wasn't sure how I felt about that. I felt safer and warmer with Harry's arm around me, so from that point of view it was nice. But his gesture was a kind of possessive one, and I didn't think I liked that. I didn't pull away from him right away though, and before I had sorted out exactly what I thought of the whole matter, I had fallen sound asleep, lulled by the dull roar of the bus's motor and the babble of voices in the front of the bus.

When I woke up, it was dark except for a few lights along the aisle of the bus and Harry murmured in my ear, "Salamanca. We're coming into the town right now."

We pulled up in front of our hotel and the driver tossed our suitcases out on the sidewalk. A cold drizzle of rain was falling out of the darkness as we streamed off the bus. I shivered as rain dripped down my neck. "I didn't realize how travel tires you out," I said to Lolita, yawning.

"Those castles and cathedrals and stuff will really take it out of you," she agreed. "What I could go for now is something totally noncultural. Say a nice warm discotheque." We staggered in the direction of the lighted hotel sign.

"Did I hear you say 'discotheque'?" said Rosemary. "You must be out of your mind. What we need is hot soup and bed."

Our hotel turned out to be a budget stop. It seemed clean, but there were little clues that it was not the Ritz. The lobby was lit by one light bulb and the souvenir shop by the front desk consisted only of two small plates with Salamanca painted on them in red. There was no elevator, and when we mounted the steps to the second floor, carrying our suitcases, we learned that the hall light was on a timer to save energy and that it didn't stay on quite long enough for you to reach your room.

Groping in the dark with the key, we finally managed to get into our room. I at once plopped my suitcase down, pushed my wet hair out of my eyes and helped Lolita get out the popcorn popper. We had just got the bad news at the desk downstairs that restaurants in Salamanca opened even later than those in Madrid. In Salamanca nobody had ever heard of a restaurant that opened before nine. Luckily, with some bullion cubes and water and a handful of wilted salad greens Lolita had saved from her dinner plate the night before, we were able to make a passable imitation of soup in the trusty popcorn popper.

Finally, later that evening our whole group trudged to a restaurant a few blocks from the hotel where great quantities of roast chicken had been prepared for us.

"My socks are soaking," I announced as I sat down at the table. Wet socks were no joke when the prospect of getting clean, dry ones was very remote. I calculated I had only one pair of warm socks left.

"Are you sort of disappointed in the trip?" said Harry sympathetically.

I looked at him in astonishment. "Are you kidding?" I said. I looked around me and cautiously lowered my voice. "Well, maybe it hasn't turned out exactly the way I thought. I didn't expect the terrorists. And I hadn't counted on the rain or on getting so tired, but really I love it. It's like being on a safari. You have to battle the elements, learn survival techniques. Notice, for example, how I am craftily slipping this bread into my purse. It may come in handy later."

He buttered his bread. "I guess I'm more the type that figures you cast your bread upon the waters so it can come back to you buttered. But I can see you're a born traveler," he said.

He was right. I *was* a born traveler. I loved looking around me and seeing foreign streets and foreign people. To me it was worth eating any amount of stale bread. It was even worth having wet socks.

Later when I was washing my socks out at midnight, Rosemary said, "How is it you always end up sitting with Harry? I thought you didn't want to be led around by the hand."

I shrugged uncomfortably. "Oh, I don't know. It just happens."

"He's a bad influence," said Rosemary. "The first time you went anywhere with him you almost got killed, and the next time you went out with him you came back drunk."

"I don't think I was actually *drunk*," I protested. "Besides, none of that was Harry's fault."

"A bad influence," she muttered.

"At least he doesn't spend hours flossing his teeth the way Trey does," I snapped.

"Girls, girls," said Lolita. "Why don't we just go to bed? I think we're all pretty tired."

I realized she was right. I never would have imagined I would sink to attacking someone for using dental floss.

Rosemary and Lolita quickly dived in under the covers. The room was far from warm, so there was a lot of incentive to get into bed. Before I could do that, though, I had to attend to my socks. After I finished washing them, I blotted them carefully with my bath towel. Unfortunately the towel was so small, thin and delicately starched that it did not soak up much moisture. The socks were still pretty wet. I was afraid if I put them in the popcorn popper and left them all night they might get overdone, so I draped them over the radiator. Then I hopped in the bed and pulled the covers up over my nose.

When we woke up the next morning, my nose, the only exposed part of me, was numb with the cold. I heard Rosemary getting out of bed. I decided to wait and see how it went before I did anything similarly rash.

"It's cold in here!" she announced indignantly. "Feel the floor."

"No, thanks," said Lolita sleepily. "You feel it for us, hon."

I heard Rosemary clumping her way across the room and finally she yelped, "The radiators! They're stone cold! They've turned off the heat."

"Probably an energy-saving measure," I said, pulling the covers up over my nose.

"This is ridiculous," said Rosemary. "If my Spanish were up to it, I'd phone the desk and complain. If we had a phone," she finished lamely.

"Would you mind just handing me my clothes, Rosemary," I said. "I think I'll just dress under the covers."

"We're going to have to do something about breakfast," said Lolita. "I think we're supposed to leave for the cathedral at nine. I think I saw a phone outside the door. Cassie, why don't you call the desk and see if they've got room service?"

I lit up. "Oh," I said. "It would be great if we could eat breakfast in bed."

Rosemary shot us a withering look. "Room service? At this place? You must be joking."

I was not joking. Breakfast is a serious matter when you know there's no lunch on until at least two o'clock. I jumped out of bed, wincing as my bare feet hit the cold floor. Sure enough, out in the hall a phone was hanging on the wall just outside our door. It had no dial and no numbers on it, so I just picked up the receiver and hoped for the best. There was a long silence, then a crackling sound and someone said something peremptory in Spanish.

"Uh...¿*Puede darnos desayuno en nuestra habitación?*" I asked. Maybe this trip would end up improving my Spanish, after all.

My brief moment of self-confidence was shattered, however, when a flood of Spanish poured forth from the phone, the only word of which I understood was the first one—"*Sí.*" I was momentarily shaken, but I soon realized he must be asking me what we wanted for breakfast. I remembered that Lolita liked hot chocolate, but that Rosemary preferred tea. I also remembered that if I asked for bacon and eggs it would be extra, but some kind of roll probably came free with the room the way it had in Madrid. After a moment of stunned silence while I calculated all these factors, I finally said, "*dos chocolates y una taza de té.*" I then hung up the phone, and totally wrung out by my efforts, I stood there breathing deeply.

"Good morning," said Harry. I saw that he was standing at his room two doors away grinning at me, and I suddenly realized I was in my pajamas. I bolted back into the room, feeling embarrassed.

"Well, what's the word?" said Lolita.

"I think they're going to send it," I said. "I hope so."

In a short while, a maid knocked at the door and handed me a tray. "*Gracias,*" I said, taking it from her. Later I wondered if I should have tipped her, but I had ordered breakfast. That was hard enough. I couldn't think of everything.

After breakfast we were careful to store away any extra packets of jam against hunger fits in the future. Rosemary's stock of Mars bars was dangerously low.

While we were getting dressed, we heard a gurgling in the pipes, and we realized the heat was being turned on again. The heat came too late to be of any help drying my socks, however. Sitting all night on a stone-cold radiator, they were just as wet as they had ever been. In fact, they seemed more wet, but I knew that had to be my imagination. Reluctantly, I took my last clean pair of socks out of my suitcase and put them on.

At nine o'clock we assembled with the rest of our group in the lobby of the hotel. One of the boys peered out the front window. "No sign of the bus yet," he reported.

Mr. Hinson looked at him indulgently. "We aren't using the bus this morning, Todd. Today, we are going to have the opportunity to walk through the beautiful and ancient university town of Salamanca." As it was freezing cold and raining steadily outside, this announcement was not met with cries of joy. Even Mrs. Hinson looked a little daunted as she tied a scarf over her head and ventured timidly outside behind her husband. Mr. Hinson raised his voice. "People, notice particularly the Clavero tower up ahead on your left. This magnificent tower is all that remains of a castle built in 1450. Soon we will be passing by the statue of Christopher Columbus."

I pulled my rain hat down farther on my head, but it didn't seem to be working very well against the fine cold rain that was seeping in everywhere. A cold wet patch was forming at my collar, and the bottoms of my pant legs were more than a little damp.

A few minutes later when we reached the statue of Christopher Columbus, I noted that it stood in a sea of mud. While I was looking up at it, I stepped in a puddle. "There go my last pair of dry socks," I muttered to Lolita.

She didn't seem to hear me. She was consulting her guidebook, which she had taken the precaution of wrapping in plastic. "Hon, did you know this town has *two* cathedrals?" she said.

"That's bad news," said Rosemary. "I don't mind it so much that the cathedrals don't have any light, but the worst part is they don't have any heat, either."

The farther we walked, the more numb my wet feet became from the cold. The streets were full of Spanish people wrapped up in furs and raincoats and bending their heads under umbrellas.

When at last we reached the cathedral and stepped into its dark nave, I had the sensation of being warmer, but that was only because we were out of the wind. There was no heat in there, that was for sure, and the only light in the vast place was cast by a small lamp near the postcard counter.

Mr. Hinson raised his voice. "We are in the Catedral Nueva, or New Cathedral," he said "which was begun in 1516." He smiled at this quaint idea of "new" and everyone tried to chuckle agreeably, but in view of how cold we all were, the jollity was a bit forced. "It is called the New Cathedral to distinguish it from the Catedral Vieja or Old Cathedral, which was built in the twelfth century." Mr. Hinson appeared unaffected by the cold, and in the slow hours that followed, we did a complete and careful tour of both the new and the old cathedral. Plus the cloisters.

"I was hoping we would be able to tour the House and Shells and the Clerecia," Mr. Hinson announced as we gathered in a large clump just inside the huge cathedral doors. "But unfortunately they are closed for restoration."

A small cheer went up from the back of the group. "And in view of the inclement weather, I think we had best forgo the one-and-a-half-hour walk through old Salamanca," he went on. I noticed Mrs. Hinson's triumphant look and had no doubt that this schedule change was her doing. "Consequently," he said, "your afternoon will be at leisure. Mrs. Hinson and I will be returning to the hotel now, and those who wish may accompany us. I remind you that your lunch meal tickets may be used at the café next door to the hotel. Others may wish to pursue the walk through old Salamanca on their own. There is a map on the reverse side of your cathedral handout sheets. Notice that our hotel is marked with an *X* on the map."

Harry grabbed my hand. "Let's go get some lunch," he said.

We were among the first to shoot out of the cathedral. After we crossed the street, Harry paused to turn and snap a picture of the rest of the wet and weary group streaming out the door with bewildered faces. He was being very good about getting pictures, and I was hopeful that there would be plenty of nice ones for my book.

"Where are we going?" I said, thrusting my cold fingers into my pockets.

"In here," he said, jerking me into the doorway of a café. It was small but it had a bar, three booths and, most important, a small electric heater beaming heat into the room. Harry deposited me in a booth and called to the man at the bar, *"Dos chocolates, dos churros, por favor."*

"What are *churros*?" I asked.

"A sort of doughnut," he said.

The bar man, wearing a white apron, slapped down a couple of mugs of hot chocolate and a plate holding a couple of pieces of twisted dough and a couple of sugar packets. Harry immediately poured his sugar packet over his *churro* and bit into it. My hot chocolate was thick enough to float a shoe in, so there was no question of drinking it. I ate a teaspoonful of it and watched Harry thoughtfully. "How come you know about *churros*?" I asked him.

"I've been to Spain before with my parents."

"You mean you've already been to all these cathedrals and museums? I would think that one time over El Escorial would be enough."

"No, we weren't up here in the north. We were in Málaga on the Mediterranean coast."

"What's that like?"

He grinned. "Warmer."

I surveyed the bill of fare posted over the bar. "Do you think we could eat lunch here? I know it's not time for a regular Spanish lunch, but I've looked up the Spanish word for snack. It's *tapa*. I could just ask if they have any."

A couple of men with fat cigars were sitting at the bar, and smoke was hanging heavily in the air throughout the small bar.

"We don't have to eat here," said Harry. "I thought we would just warm up a minute and then we could go someplace else."

"You don't have your heart set on a walk through old Salamanca, do you?" I said in hollow tones. "I'd just like to point out that my socks are soaked."

"Nah," he said. He smoothed the map of Salamanca out on the table. "I thought we could go have lunch someplace on Plaza Mayor. It's only a few blocks from here, and we have to go almost right past it, anyway, to get back to the hotel."

"Oh, good," I said. The combined calorie count of the chocolate and the *churro* must have been stupendous, but what with all the cold and all the walking I had done, I needed lots of calories to keep going, and it was easy for me to look on them as light hors d'oeuvres.

After we polished off the *churros*, we struggled into our raincoats and went outside again. Holding hands, we hurried along the shining sidewalks, dodging drips from the wrought-iron balconies high over our heads and making our way past people carrying umbrellas.

All the buildings we passed seemed to be of the same honey-colored stone. I turned to look back in the direction of the cathedral and saw its bell tower in the distance, shrouded in the misty rain. Then I twisted the collar of my raincoat up and we hurried on.

Before long we were going through one of the passageways leading to the Plaza Mayor. We stepped out of the passageway onto the big square paved with large flat stones, shiny in the rain. The plaza was edged on every side with stone buildings decorated with medallions carved in matching honey-colored stone. Even better, on the ground level it had a circular arched arcade that protected the sidewalks from the rain.

"Let's get in out of the cold," suggested Harry.

We quickly found a large and busy bar and chose a table next to its big plate-glass window that looked out on the square. I peeled off my wet socks and stuffed them in my raincoat pockets while Harry went up to the bar to get some *tapas*.

From our table next to the window, I could watch the people outside to my heart's content, their umbrellas crossing the square, blue and green and rose in the rain. On the sidewalk outside, a man in plain blue work clothes passed, wearing a beret. Next, two old ladies went by dressed completely in black, their gray hair twisted in knots at the base of their necks. At a nearby corner, a fat man missing two teeth bawled the availability of lottery tickets. I was idiotically happy. Harry was making his way back to our table through the crowd, carrying little oval dishes heaped with yellow rice. He had to inch past a mother with two small children at the next table. He plopped the rice down on the table next to our Cokes.

"I don't think they really understand bars in Spain," I said. "The bars in this country are so wholesome, full of women with shopping bags and little children. Over here they don't seem to understand how to make a bar look wicked. I miss those signs at the door telling people to stop at this point unless they're eighteen."

"You can't have everything," said Harry. "Besides, they couldn't keep kids out of bars over here. They're the only place you can get *tapas*. A kid could starve to death around here, waiting for regular mealtimes."

I prodded the mountain of yellow rice with my fork. "What's this?" I asked.

"Chicken with rice, I think. A lot of people seemed to be getting it, so I figured it was a good bet."

I scooped up a forkful of yellow rice and watched the steam rise from it. "Don't you just love Spain, Harry?"

"It's okay, I guess."

I looked at him in surprise. "If you don't like it any better than that, why did you sign up for the trip?"

"Lots of reasons. For one thing, it's nice to get away."

I sighed. "I know. It's going to be hard to get back to the old grind."

He smiled at me. "Well, don't start worrying about it now. We've got lots of time left."

I looked at him, thinking about how I had hardly really seen him properly before. I had noticed his swatch of straight blond hair, his broad forehead, but I had never noticed that faint hollow under his cheekbones or how very pale his hair was where it was cut shortest in front of his ears.

He reached over, touched the top of my nose and smiled. I put my hand on top of his.

"I wish this trip would never end," I said.

"I thought you said you were running out of clean socks," he said.

"Maybe I could find a Laundromat. All I need to make the trip is for me to find a Laundromat and to track down that movie star's kid and send Uncle Frank a terrific story."

He withdrew his hand from mine and looked over at the bar.

"Do you think this is the kind of place you leave a tip?" he said.

Moments later we were outside again in the cold. As we walked toward the passageway out of the plaza, Harry stopped before the man who was missing two teeth. *"¿Cuánto cuesta esto?"* he asked him, gesturing toward the hundreds of tickets in the pockets of the man's dirty apron.

"You're going to buy a Spanish lottery ticket?" I said incredulously as Harry handed over the required pesetas.

He pocketed the ticket with a grin. "Why not? I'm usually pretty lucky."

Chapter Seven

The next morning when we all went down to the lobby to gather for our walk to the university, a photographer was waiting for us. He carried a single camera, was dressed in combat khaki and had a cigarette hanging out of the side of his mouth. At his side was a harassed-looking woman with a clipboard who was heavily laden with camera bags and tripods.

"Just stop right there," the photographer called to us as we were walking downstairs. "That's perfect. Mandy, line 'em up in reverse order according to their heights and give me the Wilkerson kid sliding down the banister."

I started at the sound of my name, and he glanced at me. "You the Wilkerson kid? She looks a little pale. Slap some rouge on her."

Mr. Hinson was making his way down the steps with a puzzled air. "What's going on here?" he murmured. "Does anyone know these people?"

"That the tour director?" said the photographer, his cigarette dangling precariously from his lip as he spoke. "Put him in back. Okay, Mandy girl, I want a strobe bounced off the wall. Fill in those shadows over there. Keep those kids still. Okay," he said, lifting his camera. "Let's go. Oh, and tell 'em we're from *Vision*."

"*Vision?*" said Mr. Hinson blankly.

The woman with the clipboard moved over to Mr. Hinson and began talking fast in low tones, and soon I heard Mr. Hinson say, "Why, no, I have no objection. I'm glad to help out *Vision* anytime."

"Now if you'll just get up here on the banister, Cassie," she said. "Have you ever slid down a banister before?"

"Lots of times," I said. I looked around for Harry. This was the kind of thing he would enjoy. But I saw no sign of him.

"When the photographer gives the signal, I'll just give you a little push, then I'll hop back out of camera range," she explained. She produced blush-on from one of the bags and brushed a little on my cheeks.

"Okay," said the photographer. Suddenly Mandy gave me a hasty shove and down I went at great speed. I landed with a thump at the photographer's feet, doing some minor damage to my bottom and my left elbow. He looked down at me critically. "Is that all you've got to wear? Mandy, get this kid into a red shirt."

Mandy immediately ducked behind the desk and popped up dressed in her trench coat and ready to hand over the red shirt. I struggled up from the floor, dusting off my jeans. The photographer surveyed the banister. "It'd be better if she slid *up*," he said.

Mandy was clearly a woman who was willing to go far in the line of duty, but even she looked a little startled at his demand for her to defy the laws of gravity.

"I could hold her by her belt," she suggested helpfully, "and stop her midway."

"It might work," he said. "Let's try it."

Once I had changed into the red shirt, Mandy helped me climb up the banister midway. She carefully concealed herself from the camera's gaze by crouching behind Trey, and from there she reached out with both hands to hang on to my belt. I smiled and tried my best to look as if I were whizzing down at great speed, but I could tell by the expression on the photographer's face that my performance wasn't cutting it.

He looked at the banister with narrowed eyes. "What we need is a block and tackle. Then we could raise her and lower her at any speed."

"Don't forget we have to cover the prime minister's reception tonight," Mandy put in hastily.

"Okay," he said. "Let's try it again. Once more, with feeling."

In the end, I slid down the banister five times. No one complained, not even the kids who had been standing on the stairs for twenty minutes smiling foolishly. This was partly because Mandy, who was the soul of charm and tact, managed to suggest that with our cooperation we were furthering the advance of Western Civilization but mostly because everybody was dying to have his picture in *Vision*. We all meekly did just what the photographer said.

When we left at last to see the university, *Vision* went with us to photograph the entire thing. "I wonder where we could get a tame bull," the photographer muttered.

Mandy trotted along beside me as we walked, holding her clipboard in a tight grip and trying not to let the swinging cameras and camera bags throw her off her balance on the wet, slippery streets. "I'm afraid he doesn't realize that there's no such thing as a tame bull," she said, glancing at the photographer uneasily.

"Uh, how long have you been the photographer's..." I caught myself just in time to keep myself from saying "slave." "Uh, assistant," I amended hastily.

"Oh, I'm not his assistant," she said. "I'm a reporter. I do the text blocks for the story and it's my job to see that the photographer sticks to the script, the points we're supposed to cover. It's not always easy," she said, eyeing the photographer, who was walking ahead of the group with long easy strides. "Photographers can be temperamental."

For the first time I was struck by a momentary qualm about my ambition to be a reporter for *Vision*. I had rather hoped, in my future career, to rise above being a slave.

"Now tell me, Cassie," she said, "do you feel different since that fateful day in Madrid? *Vision* is particularly interested in the aftermath of terrorism."

"I feel fine," I said. "I was pretty jittery the first day or two. I stuck to my friend Harry like glue. But I think I'm more or less back to normal now."

"Your friend Harry was very supportive?" she inquired.

"Yes," I said, looking around. "I thought I saw him when we were coming downstairs. I wonder where he's gone to. I guess he wasn't that keen on seeing the university."

"Some victims of posttraumatic stress syndrome report difficulty in sleeping, loss of appetite," said Mandy. "Have you noticed any symptoms of this nature?"

"No, but to tell you the truth, hearing you talk about it is kind of giving me the creeps again."

I was still craning my neck looking for Harry. It was hard to believe he had just vanished into thin air.

We spent a good hour posing for shots in front of a huge stone gateway that Ferdinand and Isabella had donated to the University of Salamanca. I was photographed with the statue of a Renaissance friar. I was photographed with my arms around Lolita and Rosemary. I was photographed on top of a human pyramid made up of all the other kids in the group, all of us smiling idiotically at the photographer. Finally Mandy and the photographer left. I think he was still muttering about the availability of bulls in Salamanca.

We finished our tour of the historic university buildings then, but even Mr. Hinson seemed to sense that there was something a little flat about being mere tourists after having been only moments before a media event. We were all glad to trudge back to our hotel.

I looked around for Harry when we walked through the lobby, but there was still no sign of him. When we got back to the room, Lolita threw herself onto the bed and began popping bonbons into her mouth.

"Where did you get these?" said Rosemary, popping one in her own mouth. "Yum. They are scrumptious. What are they?"

"I'm not too sure," said Lolita, "but they looked good. While we had all that free time yesterday I found me a neighborhood grocery and stocked up. You may feast your eyes on the contents of my carryall," she said.

Rosemary opened the carryall and began exclaiming, "Rolls! Oranges! Yogurt! Cheese!"

"We're talking survival here," said Lolita, calmly stuffing another bonbon into her mouth.

"But how will we keep this stuff cold?" said Rosemary.

"Easy," said Lolita. "Put it on the balcony."

"I don't understand what's happened to Harry," I said.

"Have a bonbon," said Rosemary.

He didn't show up at dinner that night, either. I was a little comforted to see that his friend Mike was missing, too. They were probably off at some restaurant fancier than the ones the group went to. I was hurt that I hadn't been invited along, but it wasn't as if I owned Harry. Sometimes, it was true, I felt we were close, but then a shutter would come down over his face as if we barely knew each other, the way it had at the bar on Plaza Mayor when we were having such a nice time and suddenly he got up, ready to leave.

When we got back to the room after dinner that night, Lolita locked herself in the bathroom with her tape recorder to record a personal message to Curtis, and I carefully turned my socks over so the other side would have a chance to get dried against the radiator.

"I wonder if Harry and Mike are back from dinner yet," I said.

"Who cares?" said Rosemary, eating another bonbon. "I tell you what, Cassie, you're losing your sense of proportion."

Unfortunately I was forced to admit that there was some truth in what she said. I was spending too much time thinking of Harry.

I threw myself down on the bed and tried to concentrate on something else. "Rosemary, can you keep a secret?"

She looked alarmed. "You and Harry aren't secretly married, are you?"

I sat up indignantly. "Honestly!"

"Well, it happened in *Passion and Orchids*," she said, "and lately I've started thinking you're capable of just about anything."

"I'm not capable of that. Forget it."

"Then what's the secret?"

"Maybe I shouldn't have said anything about it."

"Oh, come on, Cassie. I won't tell anybody. What's the secret?"

I leaned forward. "Barbara Channing's son might be in our tour group, traveling incognito, of course."

Her eyes opened wide. "What makes you think that?"

"My uncle Frank said he was traveling in Spain right now, and when you think of it, have we seen any other Americans our age anywhere?"

"Well, no. But I still don't think that shows anything. He's probably traveling with a tutor or something and staying in first-class hotels."

"You get too many of your ideas out of *Passion and Orchids*. Nobody has a tutor these days. At least, I don't think so. And sending him away with a tour group like ours is exactly the kind of thing his parents would do. They're getting a divorce, they're getting geared up for a messy custody fight, so what could be better than to ship him off out of the way on a chaperoned trip with a bunch of other kids his age?''

"Maybe you're right," she said. "Who is it?"

I lowered my voice. "What do you think about Trey?"

"Trey?" she squeaked.

"Why not? What do we know about him, after all? You see, Barbara Channing's son is named Hartington Warner Cameron III. Don't you see how Trey would be a natural nickname for someone with a name like that?"

"I don't know. I just can't imagine it somehow," she said. "You would think he would have mentioned it."

"I just told you he was traveling incognito."

"Yeah," she said, her eyes opening wide. "The duke did that in *Passion and Orchids*."

"The thing is, you're in a good position to find out for me. You're the one he talks to."

"He sometimes sits with me on the bus, that's all. He's never asked me out or anything."

"So ask him about his family. How could it hurt?"

"I don't know. That seems pretty nosy."

For somebody who normally had the sensitivity of the average rhinoceros, Rosemary was inconveniently coming up with some delicate scruples.

"If we just had more to go on," she said. "I wouldn't mind so much pumping him if I were just more sure."

"Well, what do you think? What's your personal opinion? Doesn't he sort of look like Barbara Channing?"

She thought a minute. "He does have black hair," she said. "Gee, I don't know. You know how Mrs. Allison always socks us with a mountain of homework

Wednesday nights. It's been ages since I've seen Barbara Channing's show."

"If only we had a picture of her," I said, biting my lip.

Just then Lolita came out of the bathroom humming.

"Hey, Lolita," began Rosemary.

I shot her a warning look.

"You didn't mean to keep it from Lolita, did you?" she said.

"No, of course not," I said hastily. What else could I say? The truth was I wasn't keen on widening the circle of people who knew about my search. I had already let it slip out to Harry that night I drank all that wine, and I knew I *had* to tell Rosemary if I was going to get her to pump Trey, but that the more people who knew about it the harder it was to keep my suspicions from getting back to Trey, and if he found out what I was after he would really clam up.

"Guess what!" Rosemary said. "Cassie thinks Trey is really the son of Barbara Channing, but he's in disguise. What do you think? It would really be exciting if he was, wouldn't it? It's too bad we don't have a picture of her. We could compare the two of them and try to figure out if they look like they're related."

"A picture of Barbara Channing?" she said. "I think I've got one."

"You packed a picture of Barbara Channing?" I said astonished.

The lid on her big suitcase was already up and a moment later she was flourishing a copy of *Star!* "You never can tell when you're going to need a little light reading," she explained. "I like to be prepared."

"No kidding," I said, grabbing the magazine.

All three of us huddled over the picture of Barbara Channing and her co-star Race Buckner embracing on the set of her show.

"The nose isn't very much like Trey's," said Rosemary dubiously.

"Naturally not. A boy would look pretty funny with that little tiny bit of a nose," I said.

"Would you say their hair looks alike?" asked Rosemary.

"Hard to tell. You have to sort of imagine Trey's hair all fluffed out and with a pink ostrich plume in it."

"You can't tell about that kind of thing, anyway," Lolita said. "She probably rinses her hair."

"They both have fair skin and dark hair. That's something," I said. "What do you think of the ears?"

"It's kind of hard to tell what hers look like, what with the big diamond earrings."

"Just draw him out, Rosemary," said Lolita. "Ask him about his childhood, ask him how big his swimming pool is, ask him what Eddie Murphy is really like. That sort of thing."

Rosemary looked up from the magazine with her face aglow. "Okay. I'll do it. Gee, just imagine…the son of a movie star! It's just like the sort of thing that happens in *Passion and Orchids*!"

I went to sleep that night with two sets of fingers crossed. I wasn't sure I had done the right thing to take Lolita and Rosemary into my confidence. I crossed the fingers on my right hand to cover that angle. The fingers on my left hand were devoted to Harry. I crossed them hard, hoping I hadn't done anything to make him mad at me.

The next morning, we all had our suitcases out in the hall at seven-thirty. I looked down the hall and saw that three suitcases were out in front of Harry, Mike and Trey's room, but there was no sign of the boys.

At eight when we were all getting on the bus, I looked around eagerly for Harry. When I took my seat, I put my pocketbook down on the seat beside me to save the place for him.

A moment later, Trey sauntered leisurely down the aisle. He took his sunglasses off, revealing his startling blue eyes, and asked, "Is this seat taken?"

I hastily moved my things. "Uh, oh, no, not exactly," I said. I realized that I should seize this opportunity to pump Trey myself. I might not have another.

"Actually," I explained, "I was sort of saving it for Harry, but he seems to be running late."

Trey sat down and stretched his long legs out before him. "I expect he and Mike are going to miss the bus. They went out early this morning to some market. They were going to get cranberries for Thanksgiving. At least that's what they said. I warned them they'd miss the bus."

"Miss the bus?" I wailed. I looked frantically around, but there was still no sign of Harry and Mike. I had often worried that I would miss the bus, but it had never occurred to me that it might be Harry that missed it. "But we can't leave without them!"

"I think we will," said Trey. "I told Mr. Hinson what they had done and he was pretty mad."

"But we *can't* drive off and leave them!" I said.

"Mr. H. has checked their suitcases already, and he says they've got their traveler's checks and their passports and if they don't make the bus they'll just have to catch up with us."

"I can't believe he would leave one of us like that."

The words had scarcely left my mouth than the bus's motor began to rumble and we pulled away from the hotel. Trey patted my knee. "Don't worry," he said. "Mr. H. said it would be different if it were a girl. We wouldn't leave you."

I looked at him with scarcely concealed loathing. I could not understand how he could sit there smiling, when for all we knew Harry and Mike could have been hit by one of those horse and wagon get-ups we were always seeing along the road. Or attacked by a herd of goats. Or even a runaway bull.

"I didn't realize we had a celebrity in our midst," he said, smiling at me.

It took a while for it to sink in that it was me he was talking about.

"You don't have to be modest with me," he said. "I heard all about those photographs you took of the terrorist attack. No wonder *Vision* wanted to do a follow-up story on you."

"Well, my uncle's the managing editor," I said, shooting Rosemary a look. Obviously she had been talking. And after she had been sworn to secrecy. "I'd rather Mr. Hinson didn't know about it," I said. "So I'd appreciate it if you didn't mention it to anybody else."

He put his hand on my knee. "Your secret is safe with me," he said.

I wished he would take his hand off my knee.

All at once Rosemary was standing beside me. "Cassie?" she said sweetly. "Lolita needs some advice on her embroidery. Maybe you'd better go back there and help her out."

I jumped up quickly. "Oh, right. I forgot I promised to help her out with that embroidery," I said. "Excuse me, Trey," I said.

I found Lolita a few seats back occupied with a needle and embroidery hoop. I plopped down beside her. "You need advice on your embroidery?" I said.

She didn't look up. "Beats sitting next to Rosemary while steam is coming out of her ears," she said. "You better leave that girl's man alone. Something tells me she could be dangerous."

"I didn't do a thing," I said. "He was the one who kept putting his hand on my knee."

"Even worse," she said.

"I was glad to get away from him, anyway," I said. "Do you know we have actually driven off and left Harry and Mike? And Trey acts like it's nothing. Poor Harry and Mike are back there in Salamanca somewhere."

Lolita's eyes widened. "They didn't make the bus? Gosh, so that's why were were late getting off. I guess Mr. Hinson was waiting for them to show up."

"He didn't wait long, did he?" I said bitterly.

"Well, I am surprised we left them," Lolita admitted. "But I guess he felt we couldn't just wait forever. The boys know they're supposed to be on time for the bus."

"What if they couldn't help it?" I said. "What if they got gored by a runaway bull or something?"

Lolita grinned. "I haven't seen any runaway bulls yet, Cassie. I know you're upset, but you've got to keep a sense of proportion about this."

I could have stood it if people would have quit harping about my sense of proportion. I stared out the window and tried to stop thinking about runaway bulls.

Chapter Eight

It was a long drive to Mérida, and I worried the whole way. Could the boys have somehow collided with a fruit truck at the market and be buried in a heap of oranges somewhere? Or was it possible that some merchant, enraged by their low bid on his lot of cranberries, had whopped them with a stalk of celery and that even now they were wandering around in a state of total amnesia?

As we approached Mérida, the road deteriorated alarmingly. We seemed to be following a goat track into the town. How could Harry and Mike ever find their way to such an out-of-the-way little town like this?

Our bus drove into town and pulled up before a large, sprawling hotel built in the old mission style. Purple bougainvillea flowers blazed against its whitened walls. Mr. Hinson stood up. "People," he announced, "our hotel this evening is a restored convent of particular interest. Be sure to notice the cloisters and the Visigothic columns decorating some of the reception rooms. The porter will take care of your luggage.''

"The porter will take care of the luggage?" said Lolita, perking up. "I think I'm going to like this place."

When we got off the bus and stepped inside the hotel lobby, a blast of central heat hit me in the face. Obviously, if nothing else, this hotel was going to be a great place for drying socks.

Standing at the desk, we could see a leafy garden through the French doors. Rosemary peered out the glass doors. "Hey, I can see an old stone well out there in the cloisters," she said. "And they've got a canary in a cage out there. Look, Cassie!"

I cast a perfunctory glance at the garden, collected the room key and began making my way up the stairs, Lolita and Rosemary following me.

As soon as we found our room, Lolita lost no time sitting down on one of the beds and bouncing a few times. "Good mattresses," she said, "And look at that, girls! Over on the wall by the wardrobe, our own individual thermostat."

"Oh, goody," said Rosemary. "Let's set it for hot."

"Now *this* is what I call a hotel," said Lolita.

"If a person were trying to get to Mérida from Salamanca to catch up with their group," I said, "I wonder how they would do it."

"They might have to ride on a Spanish bus full of people carrying crates of chickens," said Lolita. "This Mérida place is a little off the beaten track." She looked at me sympathetically. "They're probably okay, Cassie. I'll bet they'll catch up with us in Seville."

"Are you still worrying about Harry being eaten up by a runaway bull?" said Rosemary. "Honestly, after all that idiotic enthusiasm you had about that Spanish laundry and that rusty old armor in Madrid, I can't believe you're sitting there down in the dumps when we've finally got something to be enthusiastic about. Don't you see? Central heat! Towels in the bathroom the size of sheets. Thick mattresses. And heaps of all that local color you're so gaga about. Have you lost all interest in life? Aren't you even going to ask me what I managed to find out about Trey?''

I threw myself on the bed. "All right, what did you find out about Trey?"

"I asked him if his family had a swimming pool," she said, "and they do. They have an Olympic-size swimming pool. But he said his father has back trouble and has to swim every day, so I'm not sure that counts. I mean, even people who aren't movie stars can have swimming pools, particularly if they have back trouble. I tried to draw him out, thinking that maybe something would slip out, but mostly he ended up talking about track teams."

"You should have asked him about his brothers and sisters," I said. "The Cameron kid has some younger twin sisters. If Trey admits he has twin sisters, that would cinch it."

"You didn't tell me that," said Rosemary. "How was I supposed to know?"

"It's just common sense to ask about his family," I said. "You could try to find out what his father does for a living, too. If he's the guy we're looking for, his father is a doctor."

"It would have helped if you'd given me a couple of these hints before," said Rosemary tartly.

Possibly it was only because of what I ordered for dinner—garlic soup, stewed squid and milk curd with honey—but I didn't sleep at all well that night in spite of the warm room and the good mattresses. I kept worrying about Harry and Mike.

It was pretty clear I wasn't the only person thinking about them, because the next morning everyone's suitcases were out in the hall at seven-thirty and the entire group was suspiciously prompt getting on the bus. Nobody wanted to be the next one who got left.

The bus took us only a short distance and then let us out at the ruin of a Roman theater. I had to admit that the ruin was in pretty good shape, considering how many hundreds of years had passed since the Roman Empire had been a going concern. It looked like a cross between a theater and a football stadium, with many tiers of seats and a large stage made of polished stone and decorated with pillars and with marble busts, but the whole time we were there, I kept peering around pillars and turning sharply every time I heard footsteps. I was hoping Mike and Harry would jump out on the stage amid all the busts of the emperors and shout, "We're back!" After all, they knew we had been headed to Mérida and there was positively nothing in Mérida to sightsee at *but* the Roman ruins, so it would have been a logical place to catch up with us. Still, there was no sign of them.

We left the ruins at lunchtime, and our bus headed south again. As we opened our box lunches of watercress sandwiches and tangerines, I saw we were passing fields of black-faced sheep. Soon orange trees and flowers began to appear outside our windows.

"This is more like it," said Rosemary. "Sunny Spain, at last!"

Mr. Hinson stood up in the aisles, steadying himself by holding on to a seat. "People, we are now entering the province of Andalusia. If you are alert, you may see many signs of Moorish influence. We will be in Seville in time for supper." He sat down abruptly when we hit a bump in the road.

Lolita consulted her guidebook. "'Seville is widely known as the Spanish capital of pickpockets and thieves,'" she read. She closed the guidebook and eyed her purse anxiously. "Maybe I should put my passport and my picture of Curtis in some safer place," she said.

"What safer place?" I said.

"My patented thief-proof money belt," she said, producing a strange-looking nylon-and-zippered contraption from her carryall.

"Of course," I said, impressed. Lolita thought of everything.

When we arrived at Seville, I saw at once that it was a large city of gardens and fountains. There were lovely churches and orange trees on every corner. At last, however, our bus pulled up and parked next to a neglected vacant lot. We had arrived at our hotel.

Mr. Hinson stood up. "I want to caution you," he said, "not to leave anything on the bus."

"He knows about those pickpockets," said Lolita. "Here, Cassie. I need you to help me carry a few things."

Moments later, draped with a cashmere rug, a carryall looped over my left shoulder and clutching Lolita's guidebook and magazines, as well as my own suitcase, I staggered into the lobby.

"Let me take some of that for you," said Trey, who was standing in front of the elevator.

There was barely room for Trey and me and our suitcases in the tiny elevator. When the door closed behind us, he said, "What do you say we skip the group meal tonight and go to a real restaurant?"

I breathed a silent thanks that Rosemary wasn't on the elevator with us.

"Gee, I don't know," I said.

My obvious lack of enthusiasm didn't put him off his stride for a second.

"There's a place in the old Jewish quarter that's quaint and authentic," he said. He put his arm on the wall over my head and beamed his blue eyes at me. "We could get to know each other a little better," he said.

"Oh, well, okay," I said uncomfortably.

Just then the doors swung open at our floor. "Pick you up at nine," he said.

The doors of the other tiny elevator opened and disgorged Lolita and Rosemary. "You've got the room key, don't you, Cassie?" said Rosemary.

I started guiltily. "Yes. Yes, I certainly do. Here it is. And here we are at number 442, our room. This is it, all right. Yes, indeed."

They followed me in carrying their suitcases. When we closed the door, Rosemary shot me a penetrating glance. "What were you and Trey talking about?" she asked.

I hung my coat carefully in the closet. "Nothing much," I said. "He asked me out to dinner, that's all."

There was a sinister silence. "I look on it as research," I said quickly. "This is my chance to try to find out whether he is really Barbara Channing's son. Maybe if I can gain his confidence, I can get an interview with him."

"You don't even *like* him," Rosemary burst out with a wail. "It's so unfair. Is it my looks? Is that the problem? Or is it my personality? Tell me the truth. I can take it.''

''I don't think he actually *likes* me,'' I said desperately, ''It's just that he's been all over me ever since *Vision* came and took those pictures.''

''He noticed you then for the first time,'' said Rosemary, slumping hopelessly. ''The scales fell from his eyes. Whereas before you had been only a pale, mousy little thing with no appeal and no personality, when he saw you pursued by the press he realized what a fool he had been, that you were the one, the only one for him.''

I cast a nervous glance in the mirror. ''I don't think I'm pale and mousy, do you, Lolita?''

''Hon, keep me out of this,'' she said, rolling her eyes skyward.

''Don't worry about me,'' said Rosemary with a dramatic sweep of her arm. ''I would never stand in the way of your happiness.''

''For pete's sake, it's only dinner!'' I said. I felt that if she started telling me this is just what happened in *Passion and Orchids* I was going to scream.

Room 442 definitely had a strained atmosphere until dinnertime.

At nine Trey appeared at our door. ''Hi, Rosemary! Hi, Lolita!'' he said.

Rosemary only managed a travesty of a smile, but Trey did not seem to notice.

''I asked at the desk,'' he explained, as we went down in the elevator, ''and they said the best place to get a taxi was right up on the corner at the Plaza of the Encarnación.''

Remembering the pickpockets, I clasped my purse tightly under my arm when we stepped out on the street and only breathed freely once more when we stepped safely into a taxi at the plaza. I didn't have much pocket money, and I was afraid I was going to have even less if I weren't careful.

"Barrio de Santa Cruz," Trey told the taxi driver. "That's what they call the old Jewish quarter," he explained to me. "It's supposed to be very picturesque."

The taxi took us down some narrow winding streets and then down a beautiful broad avenue past fountains dazzling with light and cascades of water.

At last the taxi pulled up in front of a large garden, and the driver began speaking rapidly in Spanish, gesturing toward the garden.

"I think he must be saying this is as close as he can get," said Trey. He carefully counted out the pesetas for the taxi driver, and as the taxi whizzed off we turned and confronted the garden. It had tall dark trees and bushes with strangely large leaves.

"This must be the way we go," he said.

I was glad to see children running around and playing in the garden, since children are rarely found playing in the haunts of thieves and violent criminals, but in the shadowy garden, I felt my old edginess returning. I wished Harry were there with me.

"*¿Donde está el barrio Santa Cruz, por favor?*" I asked the children. It was hard for me to believe this was really the right way to the barrio.

The children spoke six or eight rapid paragraphs of Spanish, and I wasn't able to follow any of it, but it was clear enough that they were pointing straight into the garden, so I thanked them and we walked on. I had to fight the feeling that the leafy branches overhanging the sidewalk were reaching for me. I wished I were back in the hotel room. I was not enjoying myself. But I told myself it was in a good cause. An intrepid reporter can't allow herself to be frightened by a few shadows and rumors of pickpockets. An intrepid reporter forges on after the story, no matter what.

Luckily we only had to go a short distance through the garden. Coming out of it, we at once found ourselves in a maze of steets so narrow that I would scarcely have believed it. We had been on some narrow streets since we came to Spain, but these were the narrowest. No vehicle larger than a bicycle could have possibly made it through. The barrio was not big on streetlights, either. Only the doorways of a few restaurants threw wedges of light out onto the street at intervals. Pausing in a small pool of light near a door, Trey pulled out his guidebook and turned to a small map of the barrio so we could find our way.

Following the map, we walked down the street a short way until we came to a small plaza, little more than a widening in the street, where a few benches stood under some orange trees. Children were running on the pavement, giggling, and a couple of college student types were sitting on a bench talking quietly to each other. I was glad to see these cheerful signs of life.

"Those kids ought to be in bed," said Trey.

"Children seem to be up at all hours in Spain," I said. "I noticed it in Salamanca, too. Uh, I guess you're used to looking out after your younger brothers and sisters, aren't you?" I said. I had realized I could turn this discussion about kids to good use. After all, the whole point of my coming out on this expedition had been to pump Trey about himself.

"How did you guess?" he said. "Yep, I'm the oldest, all right. Hey, look! That's the restaurant we're looking for over there, the one the guidebook says has 'typical Andalusian decor.'"

It was too bad the restaurant had to materialize just as I was making headway with my interrogation, but maybe I could get back to the subject of brothers and sisters later.

We went in, past the bar, to a room with low ceilings where hams, strings of garlic and turnips had been hung liberally from the bare beams and the tables and chairs were of rough-hewn wood. A tiny electric heater beamed heat at our table.

"The guidebook recommends the kidneys in sherry sauce," Trey commented, pulling out my chair for me.

"Maybe I'll try that."

The waiter stood by with pencil and order pad while we thumbed through Trey's phrase book trying to decipher the menu. At last we managed to put in our order and the waiter disappeared.

"I always get roast chicken," Trey explained. "*Pollo asado*. You know where you are with that."

"But isn't that boring?" I said.

"Nope," he said, carefully spreading his napkin on his lap. "I like roast chicken. Usually you get french fries with it, too. The Spanish don't really understand french fries. They keep letting them get in the sauce. But usually there are quite a few on top that didn't get soggy, so I make out all right with the food." He broke one of the smooth hard buns in half and began to butter it. "And now that Harry and Mike have cut out and left me with a room all to myself, I have plenty of peace and quiet," he said. "This trip is really looking up."

"Aren't you worried about them?" I asked.

"Why should I worry about them? I just want them to take their time catching up with us."

"I worry about them," I said in a low voice.

"Here comes our order," said Trey.

The kidneys I had ordered came with french fries, too. Half of my french fries had fallen into the brown sherry sauce and though somewhat soggy and brown, they were without a doubt the best french fries I had ever eaten. I wondered if there was any chance of fries with sherry sauce catching on in the U.S. If so, I wanted stock in the company.

After I had had something to eat, I found myself mellowing toward Trey. He wasn't necessarily heartless, I told myself, just because he wasn't worried about Mike and Harry. Possibly he simply had no imagination. His fondness for roast chicken rather supported this theory.

"Tell me about your family," I said. It was time to get this interrogation on the road.

"Why do you want to know about my family?"

"Don't you think that when you find out about someone's family you are finding out more about what that person is really like?"

"No," he said. "I don't. I'll give you an example. Do you have any brothers or sisters?"

"I have a brother."

"What's he like?"

"Oh, he's the usual selfish, car-crazy brother."

"See what I mean? Your brother's not like you at all, is he?"

I had to admit that Matt and I were not too much alike. Unfortunately Trey was turning out to be harder to interrogate than I thought. I wondered how it was that reporters got people to spill all those damaging admissions you were always reading in the paper.

"Well, what does your father do for a living?" I asked, ever persistent.

"What is this, the Inquisition?"

I realized I had been perhaps a trifle too obvious about my questions. "I'm writing a book about the trip," I said. "And I'm trying to get to know more about the kids on the tour and what they think of the trip."

"You're writing a book?" he said.

"Yup. You'll get a copy," I said. "Everybody who has taken the trip will get a copy, courtesy of Mr. Hinson. It's included in the tour price."

"Maybe I can help you out with that," he said. "You know, we've been in Spain for a number of days now and I've gotten some impressions of Spain and the character of the Spanish people that you might be interested in. For instance, have you noticed the way kids are allowed to stay up till all hours in this country? Everywhere we go, even at ten or eleven at night, you see kids out playing. I ask you, is that healthy? How can a country ever amount to anything if the kids don't have a regular bedtime?"

"Maybe they take naps."

"And that's another thing. The way so many of the stores close in the middle of the day, it's all out of whack with the rest of the modern world. What happens if they're doing business with a country that has some real get up and go, a country like America? You try to call them up to talk about an order or something and they're out on a three-hour lunch break."

"Well..."

"Sure, they stay open later at night, but it's a crazy system. I think we have to ask ourselves if these people are ready for a democratic government as we understand it. No wonder they had a dictator for years. The way I figure it, their moral fiber was sapped by their crazy hours. And as for this *paseo* business, it's just proof of nationwide insanity, that's all. I ask you, does it make sense to bundle up little babies and take them out when it's forty degrees and pitch-black outside? It's crazy."

"Yes, that's very interesting, what you say."

"Oh, well," he said modestly. "If you keep your eyes open, it's surprising what you can see. Just wanted to give you something you could use in the book. I have a lot of ideas. I'm always noticing things. One of these days I might write a book myself. If I could get someone else to do the rinky-dinky part, I mean. I don't want to have to fool around with getting stuff in paragraphs or checking the spelling or anything like that."

"Oh? Do you think you have the material for a book?" I said, suddenly alert. "I mean, have you *known some famous people*, or something interesting like that?"

He leaned back in his chair. "Well, that's not the kind of book I have in mind. What I was thinking of was something more in the inspirational line. I've had some terrific experiences on the track team, for example," he said. "When I was a sophomore and we were competing against Harrow Hill, Coach gave us a talking to that really turned us into winners. I'm telling you, we went out there to win, and we went prepared to give one hundred percent. It was our mental attitude that did it, pure and simple. We slaughtered those suckers, and yours truly set a new county record for the fifty-yard dash. Coach said to me, 'Trey,' he said, 'it's your mental attitude that did it. Never forget that.' I always thought that was a perfect example of the importance of your mental attitude, do you know what I mean? Now another story will show you a little better what I mean.…"

I stared hopelessly at my plate, wondering how many of these stories a person had to hear before her brain went numb. Luckily it turned out it only took two. By the time Trey was giving me an account of a meet in the spring of his sophomore year, my mind was miles away.

"Goodness, look at the time," he said finally. "Well, time flies when you're having fun. I guess we'd better get the check."

As we walked through the narrow streets back to the broad avenue where we could hail a taxi, I was not a bit bothered by the shadows and the dark streets. My mind had indeed been numbed by an excess of track team stories.

I could not quite make up my mind whether Trey was the most boring person in the world or whether all those excruciatingly dull stories about track were a smoke screen. It was hard for me to believe that anybody could be as dull as that except on purpose.

Chapter Nine

The next morning at breakfast I apologized to Rosemary. "I take back all the things I said about how it only took a little common sense to worm the truth out of Trey," I said. "I wasn't able to get a thing out of him last night."

"What did you two talk about?" said Rosemary, shooting me a suspicious look.

"Track team," I said.

She looked pleased.

At ten o'clock, Mr. Hinson gave us a lecture on the history of the Arabs in Spain, then after lunch the bus drove us to Seville Cathedral. "Consult your checklist for things to see inside the cathedral," Mr. Hinson told us. "We want to be especially sure not to miss the tomb of Christopher Columbus."

The bus stopped in front of the huge soot-blackened stone cathedral. I saw that some tourists were sitting on the edge of the fountain in front of the building, waiting for its doors to open to sightseers. Suddenly two of the tourists jumped up and waved at our bus.

"Harry!" I screamed. "It's Harry and Mike!"

We all poured off the bus and engulfed them, laughing. "We knew you had to show up here," Harry said. "They told us everybody comes to the cathedral."

"I'm glad you boys made it back," said Mr. Hinson. "You were beginning to have me worried."

I grabbed Harry's hand and squeezed it, reassuring myself that he was really there. "I'm so glad you're safe," I said.

"You must have known we'd make it back for Thanksgiving," Harry said, his eyes crinkling at the corners.

"Is today Thanksgiving?"

"Sure, and look what Mike and I have got to celebrate."

He presented me with a package.

"What is it?" asked Lolita.

"Cranberries. We had the devil of a time finding them, didn't we, Mike?"

"Sure did. Turns out they don't eat them in this country. They feed them to the pigs."

"Yeah, we finally ran into this college professor at the market, and he was able to help us out. 'Whortleberries,' he called them."

Lolita peered into the wrapped paper package. "They look awfully little and wrinkled," she said dubiously.

"Obviously, Luther Burbank did something great to the American cranberry. This is the unimproved version. But they're cranberries, all right. Mike and I tasted one."

"We've been saving our sugar packets from breakfast, lunch and dinner for days," explained Mike. "We're going to make cranberry sauce."

"How?" asked Rosemary.

"In Lolita's popcorn popper, natch," said Harry.

Rosemary cast a glance at Mr. Hinson, who was now leading the group into the cathedral. "We better get moving," she said. "They're leaving us."

"Right-o," said Harry. "We don't want to miss old Chris's tomb."

I squeezed his hand again. "I'm really glad you're back," I said. "I kept being worried all these awful things had happened to you."

"Like, what could happen to us?"

"Oh, I thought maybe you had been buried under a ton of oranges or hit in the head by a bunch of celery so you were suffering from total amnesia."

He put his arm around me. "The market was kind of confusing, but it wasn't as dangerous as all that," he said.

"It was very selfish of you to go off and have an adventure on your own," I said. "And furthermore, I hate to tell you, but I think Trey is really going to be disappointed that you're back."

"I knew you'd say something sooner or later to cheer me up," he said.

The cathedral was a vast, dark barn of a place. A congregation was attending a service in one part of it, but the place was so huge that you scarcely noticed them. Everywhere I turned I saw yet another statue laden with gold and silver brought back from the New World. Columbus's tomb was a very grand-looking business decorated by statues of four life-size kings of Spain bearing the casket on their shoulders.

After we had all been through the cathedral, Mr. Hinson counted heads. "We don't want to mislay anyone else, do we?" he said jovially. Then he led us across the street to the Alcazar, the city's castle fortress. I liked the Alcazar right away. It was like a child's idea of a fort with those neatly crenelated walls that looked so handy for shooting with bow and arrow or for pouring boiling oil on attackers.

Our guide, a pretty young woman with large, dark Spanish eyes, met us in the outer courtyard. "The Alcazar was originally the castle and fortress of the Moslem sultans," she said, "but most of what we shall see today was constructed by Pedro the Cruel when he renovated the palace in the fourteenth century. Follow me, please."

We followed her into an interior courtyard, which had mosaic blue tiles on the walls and keyhole-shaped arches giving it an Arabian Nights look. I caught my breath in surprise when I saw that real peacocks were strolling by the fountain. The courtyard was like a vision called up by Aladdin's magic lamp. Silken pillows in rich colors were piled high on oriental rugs spread around the courtyard. Near the heaped cushions, fresh flowers had been thrust into tall brass vases standing on the floor, and plates heaped high with fresh fruit lay close at hand while dark-haired girls wearing filmy harem costumes walked about aimlessly among the tourists and Spanish schoolchildren on field trips. I noticed that the girls in the harem outfits were given a strange modern touch by the assorted padded jackets they were wearing, though in one way the jackets were not surprising—the day was a tad chilly to be wearing nothing but a skimpy bolero and sheer pantaloons.

Our guide walked past a girl in a harem outfit without a glance. "Step this way, please," she said. "The palace has a most extensive collection of ladies' fans."

It was hard to work my way up close to the guide past all the kids in our group and the assorted harem dancers, but I finally managed to edge near enough to ask, "The girls in the harem outfits, what are they doing here?"

She glanced at them. "They're making a film. This one is called *Escape from the Harem.*"

I glanced at the heap of silken cushions. "Do they make many movies at the Alcazar?" I asked.

"Perhaps one every two years or so. The Moorish architecture makes it very good for films about the Middle East."

Over in a corner a bored-looking blonde in a harem outfit was sitting in a folding canvas chair while a woman worked on her crimped hair with a comb. Nearby, a man in earphones was turning a black movie camera, but he didn't seem to be actually photographing anything. The peacocks looked a little dispirited, as if they wondered what they were doing there. Golly, I thought, what a terrific picture this would make. Harry should be getting some shots of it. Where was he? I looked around for him, but there were a lot of people milling around. Suddenly, the girl in the canvas chair jumped up and called, "'Arry!" She was waving enthusiastically. I was startled because it sounded as if she were calling to Harry in Italian or something, but when I wheeled around, I didn't see him. The hairdresser coaxed the girl back into the chair muttering something of which the only word I could make out sounded like *turismo*.

Looking around me with fascination, I moved past the peacocks to where a man in a red fez and white tunic was eating a sandwich and found that I had stumbled into a small, dingy courtyard where a buffet table was set up and extras in exotic costumes were filling their plates. A plump bald man came toward me, waving his arms. "I'm so sorry, this area is closed to the public," he said. "Closed to the public, if you please."

I backed away and the peacocks fluttered their wings and moved to a safe distance. Where could Harry be? He had the most annoying way of disappearing. I looked around and saw no sign of anyone else in my group. I realized they had all gone on without me. I had better make a effort to catch up. I hurried into a room with an open door just off the courtyard. The room was full of gloomy portraits, and through the door on the far wall I could see our group in the next room standing in front of some glass cases. I rushed up to join them.

I found Harry standing in front of a glass case looking with an air of intense interest at a black lace fan. He looked up at me with wide-eyed innocence. "Amazing the things they could do with fans. The guide's just been telling us people used to flirt with them. Hard to imagine, isn't it?"

"Where have you been?" I said. "Didn't you see what a fantastic photo opportunity that was back there?"

He tapped the camera. "Got it already," he said. "Think I got a good angle on the peacocks and the fat guy with the fez. Maybe we'd better get on to those Royal Apartments or whatever. The guide seems to be moving on."

"I guess so," I said, feeling oddly dissatisfied. There was something elusive about Harry that was most annoying. One minute he was there and the next minute he was gone. It was an annoying characteristic in someone I depended on so much.

On the bus ride back to the hotel, Harry sat next to me. "I can't wait to get reunited with my suitcase," he said. "Right now I'd kill for a pair of clean socks."

I grinned at him. It was great to have him back.

When we got back to the hotel, Harry and Mike took time to shower and change, then they showed up at our door with a bag full of sugar cubes bearing the names of different restaurants we had patronized along the way. They also carried the package of cranberries. We put both ingredients together into the popcorn popper with a cupful of water.

"Are you sure this is the way you make cranberry sauce?" said Rosemary.

"It seems like as good a way as any," said Harry. "Of course, it's not going to be smooth like that jellied cranberry sauce you get in the store." He eyed Rosemary's legs speculatively. "But when I come to think of it, I'll bet we could get it smooth if we strained it through some stockings."

She primly tucked her legs under her.

"We like it with the whole berries," she said.

Lolita and I nodded vigorously in agreement. We certainly liked it better that way than strained through Rosemary's panty hose.

Harry kept tasting the sauce, and the expression on his face was not particularly reassuring. "I think we might not have had quite enough sugar cubes," he said.

Finally the berries floated on the top like bubbles, and the sauce looked thick, so we ladled some out into water glasses. "Bottoms up!" said Harry, and we all took cautious sips. It was probably the sourest thing I had ever tasted in my life.

"A bit tart," said Harry. "But it doesn't matter. Happy Thanksgiving!"

Tears stung my eyes for a second, and I had to look away. Probably nothing can make a person feel more like an American than being in a foreign country celebrating Thanksgiving. I actually found myself missing Hockley.

Everybody got up quickly, anxious to quietly ditch the cranberry sauce and put some popcorn on instead, but I sat there, all choked up, thinking about turkey and pumpkin pie, and I don't even *like* turkey and pumpkin pie. Harry shot me a sympathetic look and put his arm around me.

"I guess I'm a little bit homesick," I said. "I never thought I would get homesick."

"Tell you what," said Harry. "Why don't we go out to dinner tonight? There's this little place in the Barrio de Santa Cruz that the guidebook recommends. It's supposed to have good food and real Andalusian decor."

"It does," I said. "I was there last night with Trey."

Harry looked taken aback.

"Don't you remember," I told him, "how I was going to pump him about his family and try to find out if he's Barbara Channing's son?"

He looked at me curiously. "What did you find out?"

"Nothing much. He talked about track teams the whole time. But that's suspicious in itself. I mean, nobody can really be that interested in track. I didn't get a single bit of information out of him."

"Hey, you two," said Mike, "Come help scrub out this popcorn popper. It's a mess."

"Not to worry," said Lolita, rummaging around in her suitcase. "I think I've got some steel wool in here somewhere."

Harry got up. "I've been trying to figure out some way to help Cassie, Mike," he said. "She's trying to get proof that Trey is Barbara Channing's son. She wants to get the lowdown on his family life for an article in her uncle's magazine."

Mike was seized with a terrible fit of coughing, and Harry had to pound him on the back.

"I hope those cranberries haven't ruined poor Mike's health permanently," said Harry soberly. "I hate to admit it, but they were *more* than a little bit tart."

I looked at Mike with concern as he was still red in the face and seemed to be having trouble catching his breath. "You can keep this quiet, can't you, Mike? I don't want it to get back to Trey," I said.

He nodded mutely, coughing. "Won't breathe a word. You can count on me," he said.

Harry slapped him on the back. "You can depend on Mike," he said. "He's the soul of discretion, aren't you, Michael? Like an oyster."

Mike nodded mutely. I realized that no one could accuse Mike of being a blabbermouth. He hardly ever said anything. But I was afraid entirely too many people knew now about the hunt I had afoot.

Chapter Ten

The drive from Seville to Granada was a long one and I heard some kids in the seat behind me talking discontentedly about which of their favorite television programs they were missing. Someone turned on a transistor radio at the front of the bus, and a boy with a cherubic face announced that he had *had* it with castles and cathedrals, a sentiment for which I sensed a wide sympathy.

But when we arrived at Granada, all the complaints stopped as we all craned our necks for a look at the snow-capped Sierra Nevada, tinted pink in the sunset and rising behind the city.

The bus drove into the city and wheeled around a traffic circle with a splendid-looking monument in its center. "People, notice the monument to Ferdinand and Isabella," called Mr. Hinson.

"You can run but you can't hide from those cats," said a depressed voice behind me. "I'm gonna start dreaming about 'em next."

After driving through a shoal of cars and motorcycles in the central city, the bus began to climb up a road that wound its way back and forth up a steep slope. Twilight had come on us suddenly, and we could make out the bright lights of a few hotels beside the road.

"The Alhambra Palace Hotel, wow! That looks great," said Lolita. Our bus passed it by.

Up on our right came a less grand but still elegant-looking place, The Washington Irving. "That looks cozy," said Lolita hopefully.

The bus climbed past it and kept going up. I noticed that quite a few of the hotels seemed to be boarded up for the winter season. At last, we pulled up in front of a tall, square modern building. "Our hotel," said Lolita sadly. "El Dumpo."

The next morning at breakfast there were some rumblings about beginning yet another day with rolls and coffee. Before rioting could begin, Mr. Hinson herded us off to sightsee at the Alhambra. I wrote in my spiral-bound notebook "ctnlt. bkft. nix." to remind myself about how the kids had gotten fed up with continental breakfasts. My notebook was full of little memos like that, and I was beginning to feel pretty confident about the way my book was shaping up.

When our bus dropped us off there, I looked around me at the other kids on the tour and realized that not only were people showing signs of psychological wear and tear, but their clothes weren't in such great shape, either. All-weather coats that had begun in the New York airport as baby blue, cream and green were now the same indistinguishable dusty beige. Even the emerald coat worn by the girl with the kohl-rimmed eyes had by now given up all pretense to fashion. It had been rolled so many times into a pillow on the bus, had been spread on the ground so often on sunny afternoons as a picnic cloth, and had had so many snacks dripped on it that if it ever made it home I was sure she would have to bury it. And as for the state of my hot pink jeans, I really preferred not to think about it. There is only so much you can do with a bar of soap in a hotel sink.

When we poured into the entrance of the Alhambra, I realized we would have fit into our surroundings better if instead of being in our tired drip-dry clothes we had been dressed in filmy silks and veils, because when we stepped inside it was as if we were back in the time of the sultans.

Our guide led us through gardens with sweet-smelling myrtle trees into rooms where the walls were completely covered with tiny mosaic tiles in intricate patterns. The Alhambra was a pleasure palace like the one Kublai Khan built in Xanadu, and it seemed to trail enchantment. You half expected to meet Scheherazade around the next corner spinning one of the thousand and one tales of the Arabian Nights.

The pointed arches of the doorways and windows gave onto beautiful vistas of mountains or gardens and reflected their delicate shapes in the long reflecting pools of the gardens.

I was fascinated when our guide took us into the stone steam bathroom and showed us that little holes in the shape of moon and stars had been cut into the ceiling so the sun shining in could make rainbows in the billowing steam. Rainbows in the bathroom! It was such a good idea.

"I love this place," I said to Harry. "I want to move in and live here."

He looked around at the kids on our tour trudging past the myrtle trees with heavy loafers and expressions of infinite weariness. "Let's come back this afternoon by ourselves," he said.

"But this afternoon we're supposed to tour the cathedral."

"You haven't seen enough cathedrals?"

"You're right. I've seen enough cathedrals," I said. "Let's come back here."

Luckily our hotel was just a bit up the hill from the Alhambra, and later on it was easy for Harry and me to slip away from the group after the usual late Spanish lunch and walk down the tree-shaded old sidewalk back to the palace.

The palace was a complex of buildings with extensive gardens terraced down one side of the hill and an ancient, tall red wall thrown around the whole thing. We bought new tickets at the gate and wandered inside.

Harry stopped to take my picture in the Lion Court in front of some primitive-looking statues of lions holding a stone saucer on their backs. Then we got a passing tourist to take a picture of the two of us together by one of the reflecting pools.

"Lets go take a look at the terraced gardens," said Harry. "This place is supposed to have extensive ones." He flipped over our admission tickets of flimsy paper and surveyed the small map printed on the back. "The way I figure it," he said, "the gardens are over this way."

I followed him past some more reflecting pools and through some arched doorways until we found ourselves on a path lined with trees.

"Would you say these were *los cipréses* or would you say they are *las adelfas*?" he asked, checking the map again.

"I wouldn't know an *adelfa* if it bit me. When do we get to sit down?"

He consulted the map. "If my calculations are right, the rose gardens are through here. Want to sit in the rose garden?"

"I want to sit anywhere."

We went down a path lined with tall bushes, down a few stone steps and then, as Harry had promised, we were in the rose garden, though it took some sharp looking to recognize that. The roses were all in hibernation for the winter and showed only some thorny bare branches.

There were plenty of evergreen myrtles, however, and more important, there was a stone bench. I sat down on it, kicked off my shoes and lifted my feet up on the bench with me. My feet had put in a lot of long miles what with one thing and another, and I figured they deserved a rest. The garden was very quiet, the mountain air had a crisp, dry feel and the sun was shining warmly on us.

"I'm glad I'm not the kind of traveler that has to have the roses in bloom," I said. "I like the garden just the way it is now. Look over there. You can see the old Arab quarter of the city on the other hill. See the white buildings?"

"Yup," he said. "Cassie, I've got something to show you."

I saw he was holding out his passport.

"Your passport?" I said, puzzled.

He opened it up and I looked at it, not really taking it all in at once.

"The Secretary of State of the United States of America," it read in delicate script, "hereby requests of all whom it may concern to permit the citizen/national of the United States named herein to pass without delay or hindrance." Below that was an illegible scrawl of a signature, an awful picture of Harry and the name of the bearer, CAMERON, HARTINGTON WARNER III.

I shot him a startled look. "You?" I said. "You're Hartington Warner Cameron III?"

"Call me Harry," he said softly. "All my friends do."

I sat there in stupefied silence. It was hard for me to take in what he was telling me. How could Harry be the boy I had been looking for? Harry, who had hardly left my side since that afternoon we'd escaped from the terrorists. This was not the way I had imagined my chase would turn out, at all!

"You must hate me," I said in a low voice.

"Not exactly," he said.

"Why didn't you *tell* me?"

"I wanted to make sure the odds were in my favor first. I may be a gambler, but I'm not crazy."

I could feel my face going hot. Of course he couldn't have told me who he was. I had already told him again and again that I was ready to spill all his secrets to the world in *Vision*.

"Don't take it so hard," he said. "It's not the end of the world." His eyes flickered quickly to my face. "Unless you still want an interview."

"Oh, no!" I cried. "How can you think . . . I mean, I'd never . . ."

"Good grief, Cassie," Harry said, taking out his handkerchief. "Don't cry. It's not as bad as all that."

I grabbed the handkerchief and blew my nose. "I feel terrible that you've been having all those family problems and there I was hounding you about that interview, giving you something else to worry about."

"I wasn't too worried," he said. "I didn't see how you could prove who I was unless you got at Mike or got at my passport."

"Mike knows?"

"Sure, Mike knows. Mike's my best friend. I don't spend my whole life in disguise, you know. I mean, most of the time who cares what my mother does for a living? It's only gotten messy just lately."

I couldn't believe I had been so out of touch with what was going on around me that I had never even noticed that Harry had something on his mind. I thought bitterly about the oblivious little princess Velázquez had painted and wondered where she ended up. Probably with her head in a guillotine if she was no smarter than me.

He grinned at me. "And look, I don't expect you to pay me for taking the pictures. It was only that the way you kept going on about how much money you'd make getting an interview with me, it did tick me off some. I couldn't resist giving you a hard time."

"I don't know why you didn't just stay away from me," I said bitterly.

"You know I like you, Cassie. I mean, God knows you're an idiot, but nobody can say you're a coward."

"Thank you," I said. I realized that on the whole to call me nothing worse than an idiot showed considerable restraint on Harry's part.

I was having a hard time absorbing all the implications of the news. I mean, how could Harry be someone entirely different? It was hard to take in all at once. But some things that had puzzled me before were suddenly making sense.

"You didn't really miss the bus when we left Salamanca, did you?"

"No. When that photographer from *Vision* showed up, I figured things were getting too hot for me and I decided it would be better to get out of there. I wasn't sure how long they were going to stick around."

"You were dodging that film crew in Seville, too, weren't you? The people at the Alcázar."

"Just Giulietta. She spotted me and I had to cut out of there. She knows me because one time she came and stayed with us. My mother likes to help out young actresses. She's not the jealous type."

I looked at him and thought of Barbara Channing all covered with jewels and makeup and in a tight satin dress. It was really hard to believe that Harry was her son.

"I look like my father," he said, as if he knew just what I was thinking. I supposed he was used to people reacting that way.

I had made such a mess of things, I realized, from start to finish. It was hard to know how to apologize. How different everything looked when the quarry you hunted turned out to be somebody you knew and cared about! What had seemed like a neat adventure had gone smash for me in a very painful way. I felt like the lowest kind of crumb, the kind who would turn in a friend for a lousy four hundred dollars. Now it was hard for me to even remember what had been so attractive about the idea of getting that interview for Uncle Frank. From where I stood now, it seemed like a low and dirty trick. It had made Harry into a stranger to me. I could see that he must have had all sorts of things on his mind that he couldn't talk to me about because I was hot on the trail of that silly interview.

"Have you heard from . . ." I began hesitantly.

"My parents? No, the whole idea of the trip was to get me out from under it all. Besides, they've sort of got their hands full. It's hard for two people to fight a full-scale war when they've both got careers going."

I felt a wave of embarrassment, as if I had been caught snooping, when I thought about all the things Uncle Frank had told me. It seemed indecent for me to know things about Harry's family that he might not want me to know.

"My father does not beat up on the kids, in case that's what you're wondering about," he said a little stiffly. "My mother just plays to win, that's all, and she wants the twins."

"What about you? Who are you going to live with?"

"It's different with me. Mike's been all through this, and he says the older kids usually get to pick who they want to live with. If it doesn't work out, Mike says all you have to do is let your grades drop, steal a few things and zap, you're living with the other parent."

I couldn't figure out if that was meant to be a joke or not. It didn't seem very funny to me.

"But I guess I still keep hoping they're going to patch it up and I won't have to decide," said Harry.

"Maybe they will."

He sighed. "Not likely, really. I mean, everybody's talking to their lawyers and their private detectives instead of to each other."

I had to agree that didn't sound promising.

"To tell you the truth, it's been great to get away from it. The house is like a morgue. But I'll stay with Dad, probably. The thing is, my mother will probably get the twins and my father won't have..." He bit his lip.

He jumped up from the bench. "Do we want to see more of the garden? Do we want to look for the summer palace, the Generalife thing?"

"No," I said. "Let's go over to the old Arab quarter on the other side of the valley and look at the Alhambra from over there."

He looked across the valley. "It looks a far piece," he said.

"I'll bet we can get a taxi," I said.

We charged back down the garden paths, looking just like any tourists with nothing more on their minds than to work in another sight before dark. As we passed through the palace, I saw our guide from the morning showing another group around. *"Señor,"* I said, "where should we go to get a good view of the Alhambra from the other side of the valley?"

He smiled broadly. "Oh, Saint Nicholas church in the Arab quarter, El Albaicin. Unquestionably, the *mirador* there is the best. A three-star view. Highly recommended."

I grabbed Harry's hand and we ran out the entrance and snagged one of the taxis waiting there.

"El Albaicin," Harry told the driver.

I was glad to see that Harry was looking more like his old self. I had hated seeing him looking sad back in the garden when he was talking about his parents. I still felt slightly sick to my stomach from the shock of it all. Why did Harry have to go and be Barbara Channing's kid when we were getting along so well?

Harry looked out the taxi window. "Just imagine all the Gypsies living in those hills over there," he said. "A nice cave, a dancing bear, a fiddle and some flamenco dancing. What a life!"

"You aren't going to drop out of the tour and be a Gypsy, are you?" I said anxiously.

"Nope. I'll bet they've got fleas. I had enough of roughing it when Mike and I dropped out of the tour the last time."

We were now heading up a circular road that was going up the hill on which the old Arab quarter was perched. The road was not very wide and as we got higher up it got even narrower, and the white stucco houses crowded close against the car.

"El Albaicin," said the taxi driver, gesturing outside.

"Mirador," said Harry. *"Quiero el mirador."*

The driver shrugged his shoulders and kept driving upward. The road seemed to widen, then turned and began to head down the hill. The driver pulled up next to a large tourist bus and I saw a sign that said Mirador.

"But there's no church here," I said. "This must be the wrong *mirador*."

Harry was paying off the taxi. He looked around. "We'll find it on foot. It's got to be close by."

The taxi whizzed away. I heard the motor of the tourist bus roar and I jumped hastily out of its way. The bus drove away, and I saw that some gaily decorated donkeys, with saddle blankets of blue and red and colored tassels on their harnesses, were being loaded to carry away rubble from a demolished house next to the *mirador*.

"I wonder what *mirador* means, exactly," I said.

"Probably just means a place where you can look at something. You know, like in *mirar*, 'to look.'"

I didn't know. We hadn't gotten to *mirar* yet in my Spanish book. I moved over past the donkeys and looked at the view of the valley. "I don't see the Alhambra," I said.

"I figure it must be to the north of here, and it has to be down a bit because we're already at the top of the incline." He grabbed my hand and led me past a seedy café into a maze of narrow streets.

A little girl with curly dark hair was leaning over a wall near me. I called to her, *"¿Donde está San Nicolás, por favor?"*

Speaking reams of fluent Spanish, she gestured straight ahead. The gesture was the only thing I really grasped, but I smiled my thanks as we hurried on.

Harry cast a glance over our heads. "It's getting towards sunset. If we don't hurry, we won't get to see anything."

We began to come upon women carrying long loaves of bread and children carrying pastries and oranges. The whole neighborhood of El Albaicin seemed to be out buying supper. Around us people were laughing and talking. We passed a fancy pastry shop that was dispensing hot chocolate and pastries to customers standing at the counter, then a tiny square with a few trees and benches where children were playing. "San Nicolás?" Harry asked a man in dusty work clothes. He gestured ahead. We passed down a narrow lane and suddenly came out onto a paved terrace where some men smoking cigars sat on stone benches. A big brown dog was sitting by the stone railing and looking out at the view as if he were surveying his kingdom.

"This is it," said Harry. "Thar she blows! The Alhambra."

Sure enough, I saw the Alhambra perched on the other side of the valley. It must have looked just like this back in the days before Columbus had set off for the New World, a fortress on a hill with snow-capped peaks of the Sierra Nevada behind it, being painted a pale pink by the sunset. Even the Alhambra was blushing red in the failing light.

Harry and I sat down on one of the stone benches and watched it a moment in silence. Finally Harry said, "I'm glad you know about my family now, Cassie. Don't you think it's better this way?"

Actually I thought it was worse, but I realized there is not really any tactful way to tell somebody that you wish they aren't who they are.

When I didn't say anything, he turned to look at me. "You aren't put off by my family's being notorious, are you?" he said, half smiling.

"Oh, no! I mean, your family's not notorious. And even if they were ... But, anyway ..." I could feel myself foundering, and finally I gave up the effort to say something tactful and appropriate. "It's just that I felt close," I said sadly, "and now I feel far away."

He put his arm around me and squeezed. "Does that help?"

"I think so," I said, smiling in spite of myself.

He kissed my ear. "I had a feeling there was a cure for this problem," he said.

"Good grief, Harry!" I said in alarm. "The sun is setting!"

"Yup. I see. Very pretty."

"How are we going to get back to the hotel?"

"Hail a taxi, I guess."

"Here? In the middle of the barrio? I haven't seen any taxis at all." I looked around at the darkening landscape. "We may have to rent somebody's donkey."

"I don't think it'll come to that. We'll just walk back to the main road and flag down a taxi as it goes by."

"What if no taxis go by? We're miles from the hotel!"

"And you don't want to throw in your lot with the Gypsies in the hills?"

"I do not."

"Well, don't worry. There'll be a taxi."

"What makes you so sure of that?" I said, exasperated.

He grinned. "Have you forgotten? I'm usually lucky."

I laughed and pulled him up from the bench.

We dashed back through the narrow streets of the barrio, finding our way back to the *mirador* in the dim light only by some primitive homing instinct. The seedy cafe had come alive in the darkness and was emitting a lot of noise and music. I could see the shadowy forms of the burros, still at work hauling away rubble. Suddenly a taxi with a green light on the roof came whizzing around the curve. To me it looked more beautiful than a full-masted ship under sail. I practically threw my body in front of it to stop it.

"What's the name of our hotel?" whispered Harry as we got in.

"Gee, I don't know. It can't be El Dumpo, can it?"

"Not hardly," he murmured. "Alhambra," he told the driver. "We can always walk from there."

The air seemed close inside the little taxi and the light was very dim. It was like being in a private, safe little world as we whizzed through the streets.

"I know that back home you live a long way from me," I said to Harry.

"Where do you live?"

"In North Carolina."

"Well, that is kind of far away."

"I know we'll probably never see each other again after this trip is over a week from now," I said, "but I'm really glad I got to know you, Harry."

He pulled me close to him. "Aren't you being kind of pessimistic? Never is a long time. Also, I think you're forgetting something."

"I know. Don't tell me. You're usually lucky."

He looked complacent. "Right," he said. He reached into his pocket. "I've got something for you, too."

"This isn't another surprise is it?" I said uneasily. "I don't know if I can take another surprise."

He handed me something small and shiny. I peered closely at it in the dim light.

"It looks like a coin," I said.

"It's a lucky sixpence."

"But it's been cut in half."

"That's because I'm keeping the other half myself."

I wasn't sure exactly what it meant, but I knew that holding the sixpence in my hand I felt more cheerful. It was hard to say exactly why. Maybe the half of a sixpence seemed almost like a promise, though what kind of promise I couldn't have told you.

"There's just a little consumer warning I have to give you with this sixpence, Cassie. First of all, it won't protect you from gunfire, so don't go doing anything crazy."

"Okay. I won't. What else?"

"Also, it's no good next to people on crutches or people with freckles."

"Of course." I laughed. Suddenly, and for no precisely logical reason, I was very, very happy.

First Love from Silhouette

COMING NEXT MONTH

CAT'S CRADLE
Candice Ransom
Fifteen-year-old Romney had finally traced her nightmares back to the summer she'd spent at Chesapeake Bay when she'd been only five years old. Just exactly what had triggered the nightmares?

SPOILED ROTTEN
Brenda Cole
Everyone was surprised when pampered Brittany Allen took on a gruelling job as counselor at Camp Chabewa. How would she ever handle it?

UP IN THE AIR
Carrie Lewis
Why had Mason suddenly floated across the Grand Canyon in a balloon? Where had he come from? What was his real name? It was all *up in the air.*

KISS OF THE COBRA
Miriam Morton
How would Antha ever rescue her cousin from the danger that not only menaced her, but threatened Antha and her friends as well?

AVAILABLE THIS MONTH

A TOUCH OF MAGIC
Jeffie Ross Gordon

TAKE A WALK
Beverly Sommers

DIAMOND IN THE ROUGH
Joyce McGill

CASTLES IN SPAIN
Janice Harrell

NOW YOU CAN GET ALL THE FIRST LOVE BOOKS YOU MISSED.... WHILE QUANTITIES LAST!

To receive these FIRST LOVE books,
complete the order form for
a minimum of two books,
clip out and send together with
check or money order
payable to Silhouette Reader Service
(include 75¢ postage and handling) to:

In the U.S.:
901 Fuhrmann Blvd.
P.O. Box 1397
Buffalo, NY 14240

In Canada:
P.O. Box 609
Fort Erie, Ontario
L2A 5X3

QUANTITY	BOOK #	ISBN #	TITLE	AUTHOR	PRICE
☐	129	06129-3	The Ghost of Gamma Rho	Elaine Harper	$1.95
☐	130	06130-7	Nightshade	Jesse Osborne	1.95
☐	134	06134-X	Killebrew's Daughter	Janice Harrell	1.95
☐	135	06135-8	Bid for Romance	Dorothy Francis	1.95
☐	136	06136-6	The Shadow Knows	Becky Stewart	1.95
☐	137	06137-4	Lover's Lake	Elaine Harper	1.95
☐	138	06138-2	In the Money	Beverly Sommers	1.95
☐	139	06139-0	Breaking Away	Josephine Wunsch	1.95
☐	143	06143-9	Hungarian Rhapsody	Marilyn Youngblood	1.95
☐	144	06144-7	Country Boy	Joyce McGill	1.95
☐	145	06145-5	Janine	Elaine Harper	1.95
☐	146	06146-3	Call Back Yesterday	Doreen Owens Malek	1.95

QUANTITY	BOOK #	ISBN #	TITLE	AUTHOR	PRICE
☐	147	06147-1	Why Me?	Beverly Sommers	$1.95
☐	161	06161-7	A Chance Hero	Ann Gabhart	1.95
☐	166	06166-8	And Miles to Go	Beverly Sommers	1.95
☐	169	06169-2	Orinoco Adventure	Elaine Harper	1.95
☐	171	06171-4	Write On!	Dorothy Francis	1.95
☐	172	06172-2	The New Man	Carrie Lewis	1.95
☐	173	06173-0	Someone Else	Becky Stuart	1.95
☐	174	06174-9	Adrienne and the Blob	Judith Enderle	1.95
☐	175	06175-7	Blackbird Keep	Candice Ransom	1.95
☐	176	06176-5	Daughter of the Moon	Lynn Carlock	1.95
☐	178	06178-1	A Broken Bow	Martha Humphreys	1.95
☐	181	06181-1	Homecoming	Elaine Harper	1.95
☐	182	06182-X	The Perfect 10	Josephine Wunsch	1.95
☐	185	06185-4	Stop Thief!	Francis Dorothy	1.95
☐	187	06187-0	Birds of A Feather	Janice Harrell	1.95
☐	188	06188-9	Tomorrow and Tomorrow	Brenda Cole	1.95
☐	189	06189-7	Ghost Ship	Becky Stuart	1.95

Your Order Total $ _____

☐ (Minimum 2 Book Order)
Add appropriate sales tax $ _____

Postage and Handling   _____ .75

I enclose   _____

Name _____

Address _____

City _____

State/Prov. _____ Zip/Postal Code _____

FL-RO2B